To James,
Enjoy the magic and have,
loads of fun with Henry & Ho-Ho!

The Amazing Adventures of Henry and Ho-Ho

Dr. Bernard Shevlin

Uncle Dennis

word4word

book wizards

First published 2008

© Bernard Shevlin

Published by Word4Word, Evesham, UK
www.w4wdp.com

The right of Bernard Shevlin to be identified as author of this work has been asserted by him in accordance with the Copyright, Design & Patents Act 1988.

ISBN: 978-1-906316-10-5

A CIP catalogue record of this book is
available from the British Library.

Printed in the UK.

Please read these stories in order!

Contents

Foreword

As a full-time family doctor for 35 years, I have been constantly reminded of the stresses under which so many of our modern children live: single-parent families are increasingly common, extended family support is increasingly rare and the continual barrage of TV violence and the horrors of the nightly news conspire to make their world a dangerous and insecure place.

The bedtime story is, in many cases, the ideal antidote to our modern lifestyle, with bonding between parent and child, and wholesome stories which hark back to solid human values, at least helping the child have a peaceful night's sleep! The first twelve stories do just that, and thus far every child who has experienced them has enjoyed the stories enormously.

Then, about 15 years ago, something happened that changed my views forever. A 7-year-old was brought to me by her mother with the complaint that, "Since the next door neighbour died she is having nightmares and panics and won't let me out of her sight! Please help her!"

I really didn't have an idea about what to do, but desperate to try something I asked mother to read the little girl a bedtime story every night (from Henry and Ho-Ho) and phone me to let me know if she had enjoyed them. The report was very positive, the little girl having thoroughly enjoyed all the stories. I then set to work on a story to help the little girl (Uncle Samson's Strange Gift) with her appearing in the story and having her problems addressed. The cure was instant and permanent!

Since then I have written several stories targeting individual children with particular problems, and have had some very impressive results. In retrospect, this is hardly surprising, as the child listening to the story is in a very "suggestible" state – probably akin to hypnosis – and targeted, helpful suggestions are very likely to help.

Now I am retired from full-time practice, and the possibility of being able to help hundreds of children is enchanting. Please, as a caring parent, help me to extend this help to others. Some of the stories in part two of this book you may adapt to help your child (by changing the details about the central character to fit your child) or I will be happy to write a special story targeted at your child's problem. You can always contact me by e-mail (bernardshevlin@fenetre.co.uk) with any suggestions or problems.

Let's work together to make the world a better place!

Dr. Bernard Shevlin

Acknowledgements

Thanks to James Burlinson who worked on the original photos of Henry and Ho-Ho and must take credit for the lion's share (elephant's share?) of the illustration work. Thanks also to Brian Riley and Jan Plant for their help with supplementary picture material and Sally Hibbert for some very helpful edits.

Thanks to Sara, Peter and Sue at word4word for their unstinting support, suggestions and, above all, belief in this project. Thanks also to Alissa Robinson for her patience and creativity in dealing with my 'pickiness' about the layout of the book!

Dedication

This book is dedicated to all those wonderful and inspirational children who have allowed me to help them as their family doctor over the past 35 years. To all those children who have enjoyed and benefited from these stories and to all the children (and parents) in the future who will share in the Henry and Ho-Ho experience.

Henry Meets Ho-Ho

One morning Henry woke up feeling quite sad. "I wonder why I feel so sad," thought Henry to himself looking up at the ceiling, "After all, today is my birthday."

"Happy birthday, Henry!" said his mother, opening the bedroom door. She had brought him breakfast in bed as a special treat. Normally this was strictly forbidden as Henry could be very messy, but today was after all his birthday.

"Would you like to open your presents?" she asked. There were presents from his uncles, aunts, cousins, granny, granddad and lots of other people.

"I wonder why I am so sad with all of these presents," thought Henry again. The presents were wonderful. There was a train set, lots of books, a fire engine with a loud bell, some colouring crayons and a big stripy kite.

"Now, what would you like to do today?" asked Henry's mother after he had opened all of his presents. Henry thought for a little while. "I think I'll stay in bed, please, mummy," he finally replied. She looked at him for a few moments, wondering. Henry was a curious little boy. You could never tell what he was going to do or say next and he would sometimes seem to disappear for hours on end. Finally she laughed.

"Whatever you say, birthday boy," she said, tidying away some of the wrapping paper.

"I really can't understand why I am so sad," thought Henry, "After all, I have everything that I want."

His mother tidied all the paper into a big ball. "Oh, I nearly forgot," she said, "there is a card here from your Uncle Dennis."

From the tone of her voice when she spoke about the mysterious Uncle Dennis, Henry could tell that she was really a little embarrassed by him. Henry had never met him, but from what he had heard, Uncle Dennis was really funny and exciting, so he was very pleased that he had remembered his birthday.

"Read it out, please!" asked Henry, suddenly cheering up.

His mother opened the envelope and looked rather relieved at the contents. "Why, it isn't even a birthday card!" she said, "Just a photograph of a tree!" She turned it over.

"What does it say, what does it say?" cried Henry.

"It's only one of his silly rhymes," she replied. "It's nothing very exciting."

"Please mummy, please read it out!" said Henry.

"Oh, very well" she agreed.

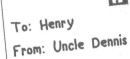

To: Henry
From: Uncle Dennis

"To my dearest nephew, Henry, for the nicest birthday dish, just go into the garden and find your dearest wish."

"What does that mean?" asked Henry.

"Probably nothing at all," said his mother, "Your Uncle Dennis has always been very wild and unpredictable."

But Henry was now quite excited, and soon put on his red shorts and sandals; he had total faith in Uncle Dennis and if he said "go into the garden and find your dearest wish" there really must be some kind of surprise in store. Henry was so excited he was beginning to forget how sad he was.

Henry had soon explored the garden; he had looked in the flowerbeds, in the greenhouse and in the rhododendron bushes, but there was no sign of his surprise from Uncle Dennis. He finally gave up and sat down underneath the old damson tree in despair. Surely Uncle Dennis wouldn't let him down? There must be another clue.

"I've got it!" shouted Henry at last, "The tree, there was a picture of the tree!" In a trice he was up on his feet and looking up into the tree. He looked along every branch, every twig and every leaf, but there was no sign of his present. Then he remembered the rhyme, "My dearest wish!" said Henry, "I have to make a wish!"

The only trouble was that Henry did not know what to wish for, and the longer he thought, the more confused he became; there was nothing that he really wanted.

He knew he was sad, but you can't wish not to have something. Finally he made up his mind. "I shall wish and wish that things turn out OK," he decided. So he began to wish.

His wishing brought lots of pictures into his mind. Pictures of places he had read about in books, stories of good friends, having picnics and laughter; pictures of adventures, the seaside and fairgrounds. Soon the tree began to shake, the branches began to tremble and a bright ray of sunshine broke from among the leaves. For a second Henry was dazzled and suddenly – 'plop' – something dropped onto the grass from high among the branches.

"My present!" cheered Henry rushing over to look at the little pink thing lying there on the grass.

"It's an elephant!" gasped Henry in surprise. Then to his utter astonishment the tiny creature began to grow. It grew and grew until it was enormous – an enormous smiling elephant – and the friendliest-looking creature that Henry could ever imagine. Henry smiled back delightedly.

"What's your name?" asked Henry, still not quite believing his eyes. The elephant began to laugh – a deep, jovial, infectious laugh.

"Ho-Ho, Ho-Ho", he replied in the nicest, jolliest laugh that made Henry want to laugh too.

"Ho-Ho? You are called Ho-Ho?" asked Henry laughing helplessly.

"I suppose I must be – you just called me that!" replied the elephant, laughing even more.

Henry and Ho-Ho could not stop laughing.

"Where do you come from?" asked Henry with tears in his eyes.

Ho-Ho scratched his ear and peered up into the tree. "I think I must live up there," he finally said. "Yes, in the trees, hanging by my trunk from a twig!" Henry laughed even more uncontrollably at the idea of this enormous elephant in a tree.

"And because the first thing I do when I wake up is to start laughing," continued Ho-Ho, "I have to let go with my trunk and I fall to the ground."

The two friends laughed until tears rolled down their cheeks.

But it was all true, for Ho-Ho could make himself very tiny as well as being a normal, elephant-sized elephant, and so he could sleep each night in the tree hanging by his trunk. Henry was very amused by his new friend. "So, are you really very big or really very small?" Henry asked Ho-Ho.

"Well," said Ho-Ho, "I'm really very big, and I'm really very small."

Both Henry and Ho-Ho found this very funny indeed.

** 🐘 **

That night Henry went to bed feeling very, very happy. It wasn't because of his birthday or because he had been given lots of presents; it was because he had been given a new friend, and though he didn't know it at the time, he was to have many, many adventures with his special magic friend, Ho-Ho the elephant.

Henry, Ho-Ho and the Stolen Silver

The next morning Henry woke up feeling very, very happy.

"I wonder why I am so happy today," thought Henry. Then he remembered meeting the magical elephant, Ho-Ho.

"It must have been a dream," Henry whispered sadly to himself, turning over to go back to sleep.

Suddenly he heard a faint 'plop'; he sat up with a start. "It wasn't a dream!" he gasped. He rushed over to the window to see if Ho-Ho was sitting under his tree, but before he could even part the curtains there was a gentle knocking on the window; it was Ho-Ho gently tapping on the glass with his trunk.

"Good morning!" said Ho-Ho, smiling his big elephant-smile, "Are you up yet?" Henry could scarcely contain his delight.

"I thought I'd just dreamt about you, and you weren't real at all, Ho-Ho," he said.

"That's what I thought when I woke up," replied Ho-Ho as the friends began to laugh.

"Well, what shall we do today?" asked Henry.

"You must decide," said Ho-Ho. "You must make the decisions."

"Right," said Henry, feeling very grown-up, "We shall go on a picnic and we shall talk and make plans."

In no time at all, Henry had packed some sandwiches, apples and bananas, and some nice orange drinks and was sitting on Ho-Ho's back going down the lane. They hadn't gone far when they heard someone calling after them: "Hey, you! – you on that elephant, stop at once." It was Patrick the policeman. As he drew nearer on his bike, the policeman smiled. "Oh, it's you, Henry. I wondered who it could be riding around on an elephant."

Henry climbed down. Behind his smile Henry could tell that something was worrying Patrick. "Is anything the matter, Patrick?" he asked.

"It's a hard job being a policeman," sighed Patrick, sitting on the grass and wiping his forehead, "Sometimes things just don't work out like they should."

"Can I help?" Henry asked. Patrick smiled and shook his head, "No, Henry, thanks anyway ... wait a minute though, maybe you can. Do you know old Miss Polly – Miss Polly Hannah who lives in the cottage at Freehay Farm?"

Henry nodded. He knew Miss Polly well and had often been to visit her and enjoyed her homemade lemonade. "Well," continued Patrick, "Thieves broke into her cottage during the night and stole all her silver. She is very upset and I'm sure if you called in to see her, it would help to cheer her up."

"Oh, yes," said Henry nodding his head with concern, "I'll certainly do that. Did you catch the thieves?"

"Well, yes and no," said Patrick folding his arms, "That's the problem. I know it is the Macwilson boys – Toby and Oliver – who did the robbery: we caught them later in Farmer Scroggins' field, but there was no sign of the silver and without the silver we can't prove that they did it. Until we can prove it was them, we can't make Miss Polly happy by returning her little treasures."

"Well, we'll certainly go and visit her," said Henry, wishing Patrick 'good luck!' as they left.

The two friends were soon at Freehay Farm. Miss Polly was sitting outside on a wooden bench, surrounded as usual by all of her cats. "How nice to see you," she said, standing up and nearly treading on one of them. "But whatever is this?" she asked, pointing to Ho-Ho, looking rather confused by the elephant who had suddenly appeared in her garden.

"This is my special friend, Ho-Ho the elephant," replied Henry. "We are going on a picnic – would you like to come with us?"

"Oh no ... I can't do that," she said shaking her head and looking sad. "You see, I've been robbed of all my old silver and the police are trying to get it back for me at this very minute. But how thoughtless of me, let me go and bring you some lemonade." She went into the house.

Ho-Ho was looking glum. "What's the matter?" whispered Henry. "I've a very good sense of smell," said Ho-Ho, "And the smell of all these cats is getting up my nose, or more exactly, up my trunk!"

"Here are your drinks," smiled Miss Polly, returning with the lemonade. Henry told her how sorry he was to hear about the burglary, and what awful boys they must be to rob an old lady. Henry finished his lemonade and soon the two friends were off again to find somewhere nice to have their picnic.

"You didn't drink your lemonade, Ho-Ho," said Henry, "Don't you like lemonade?"

"I love lemonade," replied Ho-Ho, "But even the lemonade smelt of cats!"

Henry laughed. 'I'm glad my nose isn't so sensitive,' he thought.

The two friends found a super spot for a picnic in a corner of Farmer Scroggins' field, but Henry didn't feel like eating at all; his mind was still with poor Miss Polly and the mystery of the stolen silver.

"Are elephants very clever, Ho-Ho?" asked Henry.

"I don't know for certain," replied Ho-Ho. "We do have very good memories, so if we aren't very clever the first time then we know what to do if it happens again."

Henry thought he would put Ho-Ho to the test. "Where do you think those bad boys hid Miss Polly's silver?" he asked.

"Elephants don't steal silver," said Ho-Ho laughing, "But boys do, and you are a boy so you should know."

Henry felt confused. Perhaps he should know. Here they were in the very field where the thieves had been caught, but there was nowhere to hide anything – nowhere. Just then there was a movement in the distance; it was a rabbit running for cover.

"I've got it!" shouted Henry jumping up. "Rabbit holes! Rabbit holes! The thieves must have stuffed the silver deep into the rabbit holes!"

"I thought you would know," said Ho-Ho, laughing.

"So all we have to do," continued Henry excitedly, "is to dig up all of the rabbit holes in the field and we're bound to find Miss Polly's silver!"

The two friends began to explore the field, but there were so many rabbit holes they didn't know where to start..

"It's no good," said Henry. "It would take years to dig up all these rabbit holes."

Henry was very sad. He seemed so near to the answer and yet so far away. Ho-Ho tried to comfort him, explaining that he didn't think much of silver anyway; after all you can't eat it or drink it or ride on it. Besides, Miss Polly's silver was sure to smell horribly of cats. Henry thought for a moment, then his face lit up and he did a little somersault of glee.

"That's it, you've got it! Ho-Ho, the silver is down one of the rabbit holes and it smells of cats. So all you have to do is to put your trunk down each hole and smell if it's there!"

Even Ho-Ho was finding this fun by now – a little like hide and seek, which he could never really play very well because he was so easy to find. Soon Ho-Ho was poking his trunk down the rabbit holes sniffing for the smell of cats.

The first few holes just smelt of rabbits, but on the next hole Ho-Ho

pulled a face. "Cats," he said happily, "There must be some silver down there". He inched his trunk deeper and deeper into the hole. "I can feel something," he said, beginning to pull on his trunk. Finally, after quite a struggle, out came a beautiful silver candlestick. The two friends did a little dance of celebration.

Soon they had checked all the rabbit holes and had recovered lots of silver. They put it all on Ho-Ho's back and went to see Miss Polly. Patrick was with her and they were drinking the homemade lemonade.

"You clever boys," cried Miss Polly. "You've found all my silver!" Henry explained to Patrick and Miss Polly how Ho-Ho had pulled out the lost treasure. Patrick and Miss Polly were both utterly amazed and Miss Polly wanted to give them a reward. However, by now it was getting quite late so the two friends bade their farewells and ambled off down the road.

"A very interesting case," declared Henry as they made their way home.

"Yes," said Ho-Ho, "I'll certainly remember that one." Which isn't surprising really as elephants remember everything.

** 🐘 **

"I feel so happy," thought Henry as he lay in bed that night. It wasn't just that he had helped to solve a difficult case, or that he had helped to make Miss Polly happy, or even that Patrick was so pleased with him. It was that he had found a new and special friend, and he was absolutely certain that he and Ho-Ho were going to share lots of fun and adventures together in the days to come.

Ho-Ho Learns to Skate

One day Henry woke up feeling very, very happy. "I wonder what we shall do today," he thought out loud. Suddenly there was a little 'plop' in the garden. Henry smiled, "That must be Ho-Ho coming down from his tree!" he whispered. Soon there was a gentle noise at the window: it was Ho-Ho tapping with his trunk.

"Good morning, Ho-Ho! Shall I bring you a drink on the lawn?"

"Yes please," replied Ho-Ho, stretching. "It's been a long night." In no time at all the two friends were sitting on the lawn underneath Ho-Ho's tree, drinking orange juice.

"What shall we do today?" asked Henry. Ho-Ho smiled; he wasn't the sort for making decisions. "What would you like to do?" he replied. Henry thought for a minute. "Well, more than anything in the world, I'd like us to go to the seaside, but I know that's impossible, Ho-Ho."

"I'd like to go to the seaside too," said Ho-Ho. "I've seen pictures of the seaside and it looks like a lot of fun."

"The seaside is wonderful," added Henry. "But we have no way of getting there. It's miles too far to walk and I couldn't take you on the train."

Henry couldn't help laughing at the thought of taking the enormous elephant on the train.

"What is the fastest a boy can travel?" asked Ho-Ho, smiling as always when faced with an impossible problem. Henry thought for a moment; "Running," he finally said, "Running, cycling or roller skating."

"What is roller skating?" asked Ho-Ho.

Henry could not believe his wise old friend had never heard of roller skates. In a trice he rushed into the garage and brought out a couple of old pairs. Quickly he strapped on his favourite blue pair and began skating up and down the drive, falling over several times in the process. Ho-Ho was helpless with laughter and had giant tears rolling down his enormous cheeks.

Finally he could speak again. "What an amazing and wonderful way to travel; may I try?" At this, Henry burst out laughing. The idea of an elephant roller skating was just too silly for words.

"Anyway, Ho-Ho where would you find roller skates big enough for you? These are far too small."

"Hmm," said Ho-Ho thoughtfully. "Perhaps the roller skates are too small for me, or perhaps I am too large for them!" The two friends looked at each other, though Henry had no idea what the jolly elephant meant. Then, to Henry's astonishment, Ho-Ho began to shrink. In front of his very eyes the amazing creature became smaller and smaller and smaller until he was the perfect size to fit into the roller skates.

Eagerly the two friends strapped a roller skate onto each of Ho-Ho's feet and Ho-Ho began to 'skate' – one of the strangest sights imaginable. He fell onto his head, his back, his side; he rolled over into the potato patch and into the hedge, he tumbled into the compost heap ... Henry was beside himself with laughter. Indeed for many months afterwards, Henry could always cheer himself up by remembering that morning when Ho-Ho learned to skate.

"Well, that's it," said Ho-Ho finally. "I can now roller skate." He stood up and attempted a little bow, which unfortunately made him fall over into the rhubarb. The two friends dissolved again into tears of laughter.

When he had recovered, Henry made a startling discovery; "Ho-Ho, you're back to your normal size, and look, the roller skates still fit you perfectly! They somehow grew with you when you came back to your normal size!"

** ** **

"How very fortunate," said Ho-Ho, "Perhaps we can go to the seaside after all!"

The journey went very quickly, in spite of a couple of mishaps and Henry having to explain about having to stop when the traffic lights are on red.

Ho-Ho was certainly an excellent roller skater. The sun was shining as the two friends arrived at the seaside. They played in the sand, went paddling in the sea and had some candy floss and ice-cream. Unfortunately they hadn't got enough money to buy a bucket of ice-cream, and that's what Ho-Ho really wanted to cool him down after skating all that way, so they had to settle for something smaller!

Just then Henry heard a lady crying. She seemed to be very upset and was explaining her problem to a policeman.

"I'd just accepted the ring from Arthur," she said, "When that crazy seagull swooped down and took it from my hand!" She pointed to a rocky cliff where a seagull had flown. Henry could even see the ring glistening in the sun, but the cliff was so steep, recovering the ring looked impossible. Henry felt very sorry for her, and he and Ho-Ho decided to help.

They went down to the bottom of the cliff where the seagull had her nest. Even though the cliff was extremely steep, Henry had a go at climbing. But it was hopeless; there just seemed to be no way to rescue the lost ring.

"Have you any ideas, Ho-Ho?" asked Henry.

"We just need something enormously long to reach it," said Ho-Ho. Henry was disappointed; was that the best suggestion his wise old friend could think of?

"The longest thing around here is your trunk," said Henry, "but even that is far too short."

"Yes," said Ho-Ho, "Besides, I'm so hot I feel like I'm melting!" Henry thought for a moment. He didn't know very much about normal elephant's trunks, never mind magic ones, but surely, if he were very hot, it might stretch further than normal. Ho-Ho listened to Henry's theory and decided to give it a try. He stood at the foot of the cliff and stretched up as far as he possibly could. Then he began to reach up with his trunk. At first it looked very silly as the distance was far too great, but after some effort the trunk began to stretch – just a little at first, but then more and more.

"Imagine it's getting longer still," cried Henry. "If you can learn to roller skate, you can certainly learn to stretch your trunk!" Ho-Ho was so proud remembering how he had learned to skate; he puffed with pride and his trunk grew even more, until it was able to dip into the seagull's nest and take the ring.

The lady could not believe her eyes when the small boy and his friend returned her ring. She really would have given them anything they had asked but there was only one thing that a very hot elephant with a sore overstretched trunk wanted – a bucket of ice-cream! Even Henry was impressed by the mess that Ho-Ho made with his 'reward'; he sloshed it in his eyes, his ears and over his head. All the children came to see the happy elephant eating his bucket of ice-cream. They all had a wonderful time.

** **

That night in bed Henry smiled to himself. What a wonderful day it had been: Ho-Ho had learnt to roller skate, they had been on a wonderful trip to the seaside, they had found the lady's ring and received a bucket of ice-cream as a reward. He was exhausted by his adventures and it wasn't long before he was sound asleep dreaming of tomorrow.

Henry and Ho-Ho and a Strange Thief

Ho-Ho was sleeping soundly, upside down, hanging by his trunk from a very high twig in his tree. Even in his sleep he wore a happy smile. Then, through his dreams came sounds of music. Ho-Ho began to waken. As he began to waken he began to laugh, making his trunk uncurl from around the twig. As the trunk uncurled he began to fall, until finally – 'plop' – he landed on the soft grass below. At once he began to grow from the tiny, pink curled-up elephant into an enormous laughing elephant.

"Ho-ho, ho-ho, ho-ho," he laughed.

"Good morning, Ho-Ho," said Henry smiling.

"Where's the music coming from?" asked Ho-Ho.

"It's a present I had for my birthday," said Henry. "It's called a transitory radio – or something like that. You can hear all kinds of things on it."

Ho-Ho was delighted. He asked Henry to turn the radio louder, and then softer, and then to tune it in to different radio stations. He didn't much care for all the talking, but he loved all the music. He was so happy with the discovery he did a little dance.

"This is most wonderful," said Ho-Ho, his eyes open wide with delight. "Can we take it with us on today's adventure?"

"Certainly," said Henry, "In fact we ought to be off by now."

The two friends strapped on Ho-Ho's roller skates and they were soon speeding along the roads to their favourite seaside town. Ho-Ho loved to hear the music play as he skated along, though he had to stop himself from doing a little dance at the traffic lights. Even on the beach, Ho-Ho wanted to keep the music switched on – but not too loud, so it didn't disturb other people. Henry thought it was about time to go and buy them an ice-cream, so he left Ho-Ho to listen to some brass-band music, which he greatly enjoyed.

"Two tubs of ice-cream, please," Henry asked the ice-cream man, adding how beautiful the beach looked in the sun.

"Yes indeed," said the man, "There should be a lot more people around than this." He leaned over and whispered in Henry's ear, "It's the thieves that stop folks coming, you know."

Henry was most curious about the 'thieves' and asked the ice-cream man to tell him more. It seemed that over the past month, people had been losing things on the beach – some quite unusual things, such as deck chairs, beach-balls, sun-hats and parasols; someone had even lost a pet canary! (Though what they were doing with a pet canary on the beach is another question.)

"I hope you don't have any valuables worth stealing," finished the ice-cream man, looking concerned.

Henry shook his head. There was only his radio, and surely nobody would steal from an elephant. While taking the ice-creams back to Ho-Ho, Henry began to think about this mystery. Who would want to steal a canary, or deck chairs ... it was certainly most odd. When he arrived back, Ho-Ho was fast asleep, in a normal-sized daytime sleep.

"Wake up for your ice-cream," said Henry.

Ho-Ho opened his eyes, smiling.

"Put the music back on please, Henry," asked Ho-Ho.

Then Henry noticed: his radio was gone! The two friends looked around but there was no sign of it. Then Henry remembered the warnings of the ice-cream man, and explained all he knew about the thieves to Ho-Ho.

"What shall we do?" asked Henry. Ho-Ho thought for a minute.

"If something is lost, you should look for it," he finally said. Henry was unimpressed, but had no better ideas himself, so the two friends began to explore the beach looking for the missing radio. They searched for hours but could see no sign of it. It looked hopeless and Henry was beginning to despair when suddenly Ho-Ho began to dance.

"Why are you dancing?" asked Henry, "We're supposed to be looking for the radio."

"It's that nice music," said Ho-Ho, "I just feel like dancing when they play that."

Henry listened but could hear nothing – nor could he see any possible place where the music could be coming from.

"Where is the music coming from?" asked Henry curiously, forgetting his worries for a moment.

"I'll show you," said Ho-Ho, "Just follow me."

Ho-Ho led the way. Henry was amazed at how sharp Ho-Ho's hearing must be. He finally did hear it, and it seemed to be coming from inside a cave.

"It's coming from in there," said Ho-Ho confidently.

The cave opening was quite small – far too small for a large elephant, so Henry put his head inside. He nearly yelled with fright, for there was the biggest, most evil-looking monster of an octopus that he had ever seen; he only just moved away in time before one of the giant tentacles moved in his direction. He did, however, have time to see where the music was coming from; it was his own transistor radio! So here was the thief. Henry discussed the problem with Ho-Ho, but neither of them had any idea what to do.

"Something may turn up," said Ho-Ho yawning. "I feel so sleepy though when they play this type of music." The radio was playing a lullaby and a sudden thought struck Henry. He peeped again into the cave; the octopus's eyes were shut.

"Quick," said Henry, "reach your trunk into the cave and rescue the things that have been stolen – but save the radio until last – we don't want him to wake up!"

So, Ho-Ho set to work. He pulled out several deck chairs, a pair of sunglasses, some parasols and umbrellas, a canary cage, three teddies, five dolls, a billiard cue and a tin of cat food, among many other things. For a moment the octopus had stirred, but he thought that Ho-Ho's trunk was just one of his tentacles. Last of all Ho-Ho pulled out the transistor radio. By now a crowd had gathered, including the local policeman.

"We've found your thief," said Henry, pointing to the cave. "It's a giant octopus, and all these things were hidden in there."

The policeman was delighted and arranged for all of the property to be returned to its rightful owners.

"I suppose I'd better give you detectives a reward," he concluded with a wink, "You've certainly earned it!" Now, for a hot elephant on a beach there was only one possible reward, of course – a bucket of ice-cream. Ho-Ho really didn't mind eating it in front of all the children, who found the sight of him sloshing ice-cream all over himself hilariously funny.

That night in bed Henry felt especially happy. He and Ho-Ho were certainly very good at solving mysteries. Perhaps he would be a proper detective when he grew up. Either that or a fireman. But he still did want to drive a train, or perhaps one of those big lorries with a trailer behind ... There were so many things to do. Henry was soon fast asleep, with a happy smile on his face.

Henry and Ho-Ho: Donkey in Distress

Henry and Ho-Ho were having a morning orange drink underneath Ho-Ho's tree. "We have helped such a lot of people these last few weeks," said Henry, "And it has been fun doing it. Especially with you to advise me, Ho-Ho."

Ho-Ho nodded; he had enjoyed himself enormously as well. If only life could carry on just like this ... but where would they be able to keep finding people who needed help? So far all their adventures had happened so naturally – without trying at all.

"Let's go to the seaside!" said Ho-Ho suddenly. It was most unlike Ho-Ho to suggest anything; he normally just waited for Henry to make the decisions. "You see," he continued, "I just have a feeling that we might be needed there."

That was more than enough for Henry. In no time at all, they had strapped on Ho-Ho's giant roller skates and were speeding towards the seaside. They were more than half way when Henry spotted a strange sight at the side of the road. It was a cart piled high with belongings. The donkey who had been pulling it had been released from his harness and was lying at the side of the road. A kindly-looking man and his daughter were patting the animal's head, and the little girl was in tears.

"Whoa!" shouted Henry, but Ho-Ho had already spotted the trouble and was slowing down to investigate.

"There, there, old girl," the man was saying to the poor old donkey. "It'll be all right, you'll see."

It made Henry and Ho-Ho very sad to see the little girl crying and the donkey so sad and poorly.

"I'm Henry and this is my friend Ho-Ho," said Henry, "Can we be of service?" (Henry had heard someone on the radio say 'can I be of service' and thought it sounded rather grown-up).

"I don't think you can," said the man, sighing deeply. "You see, we are on our way to Southpool but our poor donkey just can't go any further; she is just totally exhausted. I really don't know what you can do, but we must be on time for our new job."

Henry looked at the old donkey. "You're sure she isn't ill or something?" he asked.

The man smiled and shook his head. "Oh no, she isn't ill – and I should know. Let me introduce myself," the man continued, "Harry Biggins and this is my daughter Fiona. I'm an animal trainer and we're just going to my new job at the circus in Southpool." Henry and Ho-Ho whispered together for a few minutes; they both had the same idea.

"What we must do," said Henry feeling very grown-up, "Is for you and your daughter to travel on Ho-Ho's back with me and we'll put your donkey in the cart and tow her along behind!" Harry was delighted, though he did make Ho-Ho promise not to go too fast as he had never seen an elephant on roller skates before!

Henry, Harry and Fiona had a nice long chat during the rest of the journey and Henry found out lots of interesting things about these nice people. Harry probably knew more about donkeys than anyone else in the world and Fiona wanted to become a tightrope walker when she grew up. All too soon, Henry and Ho-Ho were dropping off their new friends at the circus, which was quite near the beach.

"Well, that was our good deed for today!" said Henry.

"Perhaps," said Ho-Ho, hot and smiling, "But you never can tell."

** ** **

On the beach, Ho-Ho was soon fast asleep, but Henry was wide awake. He had enjoyed talking to Harry and Fiona so much that he was keen to meet new friends and have some fun. He walked up and down the sands trying to make friends and talk to other children, but they were all far too shy.

"I wonder why they don't like me?" muttered Henry to himself, quite unable to understand their shyness. As he returned to his sleeping friend, he heard some children shouting and complaining to the donkey-ride man.

"Your donkey is lazy," they shouted, "He won't gallop and give us proper rides. We want our money back."

Just then Harry and Fiona arrived. Henry brightened up immediately and began to tell them about the unfriendly children on the beach and how they were being unkind to the poor donkey. Harry shook his head as he looked at the unpopular animal, who was called Jack, and was a very good and hard-working donkey normally.

"The trouble is that the poor donkey is too hot; if he had a straw hat he would have far more energy and give the children better rides," Harry told Henry.

Harry felt very sorry for the donkey; after all, his own donkey had been in a similar state a few hours earlier.

"If the man would let me," Harry said, "I'd take that poor donkey and buy him a straw hat myself!"

Henry looked at Ho-Ho, who was awake and listening by now.

"I bet that the man won't let the donkey go for a hat," said Henry, "Because then he would be gone for an hour or more and that would mean that he would lose money. Unless ..."

Henry and Ho-Ho looked at each other and gave a knowing wink; they had just had the same idea for the second time that day. They went up to the donkey-ride man and explained why Jack was not feeling well and how their friend Harry would take him for a straw hat.

"What about the money I'd be losing?" growled the man.

"My friend Ho-Ho will give the children rides while the donkey finds a good hat!" said Henry, solving the problem in a single stroke.

For the next hour or so Ho-Ho gave the children rides. They all loved it and were so nice to Henry, who had to ride with them as the man was frightened of elephants. All the children were very curious about Henry and some offered to buy him an ice-cream. Far too quickly Harry returned with Jack who was all dressed up in a very comical straw hat. The children all laughed and wanted to ride on him, and being cooler he gave them much better rides than before. The man was so pleased about how things had worked out that he offered to buy the friends whatever they wanted ... And to a hot elephant on a hot beach, there was only one thing in the world – a big bucket of ice-cream.

Going home that night Henry was very happy indeed; they had made lots of friends, they had helped Harry and Fiona and made two donkeys much happier.

"It's really nice helping people," Henry whispered in Ho-Ho's ear.

"Yes, especially when there's a bucket of ice-cream too!" said Ho-Ho. The two friends laughed contentedly as the sun slowly dropped behind the horizon.

Ho-Ho's Magic Button

Henry and Ho-Ho were sitting under the damson tree. Henry was looking rather puzzled. "How do you make yourself go so small, Ho-Ho?"

Ho-Ho smiled and looked very mysterious. "I have a magic button on my forehead," he said. Henry looked at Ho-Ho's forehead with great curiosity and sure enough there was the little button, which he had somehow never noticed before.

"When I press it with my trunk, I become the small pink elephant that can float back up into my tree," he added.

"Can I press it?" asked Henry.

Ho-Ho thought for a while. "Yes," he said finally, "I think that will probably be all right."

Very, very nervously, Henry reached up and touched the button on Ho-Ho's forehead. At first nothing happened, but then he pressed a bit more firmly and lo and behold the huge elephant shrank to the size of a tiny, tiny mouse.

Henry was mightily impressed. "Please make yourself normal size again now, Ho-Ho," Henry asked. After a few moments there sat the huge smiling elephant once again. Henry was thrilled with this discovery; to him it seemed like magic!

"Let's do it again. Please let me do it again," he cried. Ho-Ho reluctantly agreed. Henry made Ho-Ho go big and small several more times, and each time he was totally delighted with the result.

Eventually Ho-Ho became quite weary with the game and said: "I am getting very tired with all this shrinking down and growing big. I think I may need a sleep up in my tree to restore my energies! Bye, Henry!" And with that, Ho-Ho disappeared.

"Oh dear, I shouldn't have tired out my friend," Henry murmured, realising that he would now have to wait until Ho-Ho had recovered his strength before they could start their adventures.

"I'll go and get us some orange juice for when he wakes up," he decided finally. Henry wandered down to the kitchen feeling a little glum and guilty for exhausting his friend.

As he opened the kitchen door his mother looked rather frightened and held a finger to her lips. "Shhh," she whispered to Henry, taking his hand and leading him back outside and into the garden, "Trixie is asleep and mustn't be disturbed," she said.

Henry had heard about this girl called 'Trixie', having accidentally listened in on some grown-up conversations. He remembered them saying that she was a 'spoilt only child' and a 'troublesome teenager', and though he didn't quite know what those were, he was happy that he probably wasn't either of them.

"She will only be staying for a few days," continued his mother, "Just so that her poor family can have a break."

His mother noticed the puzzled look on Henry's face. "She is a very difficult young lady," his mother continued, "Who has fallen into bad company, and she really does need to be looked after until she recovers."

"Recovers from what?" asked Henry, now more puzzled than ever.

"Henry, you are not old enough to understand, but Trixie made some very bad friends and she has been taking things called drugs, which affected her mind. So we must all take turns in looking after her until she gets better."

Henry didn't think that would be too bad as a 'young lady', especially a 'teenager', wouldn't want to bother with a young boy; she would hopefully just leave him in peace to have his adventures with his friend Ho-Ho.

Just then Trixie appeared. His mother froze and seemed very nervous.

"Are you all right?" she finally said. Trixie ignored the question and just looked from Henry to his mother.

"This is my son, Henry," was finally said by way of an introduction. Henry's mouth hung open in amazement, but he finally held his hand out to shake Trixie's hand.

"Why is your face all white?" he finally asked. "Are you a Martian?" Henry had heard of people from other planets who looked very different from us but didn't know whether they really existed or not.

"I'm so sorry," said his mother quickly, "Henry doesn't know much about teenagers and make-up!" she added apologetically.

"I am a Trojan," Trixie finally announced with a tone of disbelief, amazed that even a young boy would not know the significance of her dress and make-up.

"What's a Trojan?" asked Henry, wrinkling his nose.

Trixie looked up at the sky and shook her head in despair, obviously feeling that she should not have to answer such silly questions.

"Me and all my friends dress like this, because we are different. We dress in black and do our faces white because the world is black."

"It's a special club, you see, Henry – a sort of gang. They go to the same places together and do the same sorts of things," his mother added quickly.

Henry was very glad that he wasn't old enough to join the 'gang' as Trixie seemed very grumpy and rude and he didn't want to dress in black and paint his face white.

They made their way into the house and decided to have an early lunch. Henry was feeling a little peckish and the promise of some homemade soup was very attractive.

However, this soup was like none he had ever had before; it was horrible! His mother noticed the expression on his face.

"I made this soup especially for Trixie," she explained, "As there are a lot of foods which she cannot eat."

The story slowly emerged that Trixie suffered from all kinds of health problems with strange things called 'allergies'. For instance she was allergic to milk, eggs, meat and fruit, so when she ate them she became ill and sneezed a lot; in fact there was very little that Trixie was not allergic to!

Poor Henry had to share in her strange food choices and it soon became clear that a lot of his favourite foods would not be available while Trixie was around – things like chocolate, fruit, jelly, trifle and various other treats; life had certainly taken a turn for the worse! Then came the bombshell: "I really like this food and being here; I think I'll stay for a few weeks ... maybe even longer!" Trixie said. (She was a very ill-mannered girl and didn't even ask if it would be all right for her to stay longer!)

The days dragged on, with no sign of Trixie wanting to leave. What upset Henry the most, however, was the fact that he had difficulty in getting outside and under the damson tree to talk to Ho-Ho. Trixie always seemed to be around wanting to talk to him and in need of his company. After a few days, Henry had visited his friend just the once, for Trixie would not leave him alone. She talked all the time about her friends, who were all 'Trojans' like her. She told Henry how they had danced and had taken these 'drugs', which made them feel happy but had muddled Trixie's brain so that she couldn't tell what was real and what was imaginary! It amazed Henry that she would have friends like that; real friends – like Ho-Ho – would always protect you and rescue you from such silliness.

While she was talking, Henry's mind would wander, remembering good times with Ho-Ho and dreaming about adventures that lay in store for the future. Trixie hardly noticed; she was only interested in herself and her own little world.

"Then I started imagining things and I knew that I had to go home and settle myself down," Trixie was saying.

"What kinds of things did you imagine?" asked Henry, yawning.

"All kinds of things, but especially animals. Now I know that I am better and nearly ready to go back to my Trojan friends, but if the imaginings came back I would have to go back home and get some help."

"But how would you know if they were real or just in your mind?" Henry asked, as a dark plan began to appear at the back of his mind, adding: "Have you ever imagined elephants?"

"Well there aren't any elephants around here, so if I saw one, it would certainly be imagined. So if, for instance, I imagined an elephant in that big tree down there, I would know I must go back home at once!"

"I must go for a walk on my own," said Henry, "I am getting a headache from all this talking."

** **

Henry had a rather strange idea of how to make Trixie leave, but he felt a bit guilty as, after all, she did have a lot of problems. On the other hand, this surely wasn't an ideal place for her, with only Henry and his mother for company.

Then one morning while having breakfast, things became even more desperate.

"Although I feel very well in myself," Trixie was telling Henry's mother, "I do think my allergies are worse. I think that my bedroom is full of allergies which I am breathing in," she said, turning pitifully to Henry's mother. "I think I need to change bedrooms," she added.

"Well there is only one other available bedroom in our house," said Henry's mother, "And that is Henry's bedroom. However, I'm sure that Henry wouldn't mind swapping bedrooms with you."

She looked at Henry with a very stern expression and Henry knew that he had no choice but to change bedrooms.

For Henry, that was the last straw. His life had changed from a series of happy adventures into something quite horrible, with horrible food and little chance of meeting with his friend Ho-Ho, and now he was going to have to give up his own bedroom! He would never hear that wonderful sound of Ho-Ho tapping on his window with his trunk so long as Trixie stayed at their house.

However, if Trixie could somehow see Ho-Ho up the tree, she had promised that she would leave and go back to her own home, which would solve all his problems! His feelings of guilt at the plan totally disappeared; the more he thought about it the more sense it made.

The next day Henry's mother took Trixie into town on some kind of shopping trip. Henry seized his chance to be with Ho-Ho and soon the two friends were talking under the damson tree.

"So all you have to do, Ho-Ho, is to climb up the tree," Henry finished.

"But I am afraid of heights," said Ho-Ho, "and I can't climb anyway!"

"But you sleep up in the tree every night!" objected Henry.

"That is different," said Ho-Ho, looking very wise.

"When I am the small, asleep, pink elephant I am very light and happy in the tree. But when I am the big, grey, awake elephant, I am very scared of them!"

The two friends sat in silence for a while. The situation was certainly desperate. Henry's face suddenly brightened.

"I've got it!" Henry announced happily. "We'll use your magic button to shrink you down to a small size and then I'll climb up the big old tree with you in my pocket. Then you can peep out and you will see that there is nothing to be frightened about from being high up! Then after that I can teach you to climb!"

Ho-Ho looked doubtful and needed a lot of persuading from Henry, but eventually he agreed. They made their way to the oak tree at the bottom of the garden. This was an extremely big old tree that was very safe for climbing and Henry had climbed it many times in the past.

Soon, with Ho-Ho shrunk down to his small size, Henry was climbing the tree. This time he climbed higher than he had ever done before. The view was indeed magnificent and when he showed Ho-Ho, holding him tightly in his hand, Ho-Ho was also very impressed. Indeed the views were so beautiful that Henry lost all sense of time and several hours passed without the two friends even noticing.

Meanwhile, Trixie and Henry's mother had returned home from their shopping trip. Trixie seemed rather distressed and was even worrying about where Henry might be.

"Why don't you go and find Henry?" said his mother. Even she seemed to be becoming irritated by Trixie's continuing demands. "He can't be far away; he must be somewhere in the garden."

Trixie went out and looked around the garden, calling out Henry's name. Eventually she went down to the far end of the garden where the big old oak tree stood. Henry had dozed off to sleep and was startled to hear Trixie calling him. At first he forgot where he was, but then it all came flooding back. His first concern was for Ho-Ho and he reached in his pocket to find him. Unfortunately in his haste he must have accidentally touched the button on Ho-Ho's forehead and immediately the little elephant grew bigger and bigger and bigger. The tree began to creak and groan under the enormous weight and very soon, a huge smiling elephant was stretched across the mighty oak tree's branches. Trixie screamed when she saw the elephant in the branches of the tree and ran straight into the house.

Henry was startled by the scream and for some reason felt very guilty. He was sure that his mother would blame him for Trixie's fright. He pressed on

Ho-Ho's magic button and put the small elephant into his pocket. He climbed down the tree and walked slowly back across the lawn to the damson tree. He pressed on Ho-Ho's button again and the elephant grew back to his normal size. The two friends discussed what had happened.

"I still don't think I can climb trees," said Ho-Ho, "But the view was absolutely beautiful and it was so nice of you to show it to me. Perhaps we can do it again sometime?"

It had been a wonderful experience to have shared with his special friend and overall Henry was pleased that they had had the climbing adventure. Soon the two friends said their farewells and Ho-Ho went back up his tree, while Henry trudged down to the house, fearing the worst.

** 🐘 **

When he arrived Trixie was nowhere to be seen. "Where's Trixie?" Henry asked, hoping his mother wouldn't suspect anything.

"Henry, you must try to understand that Trixie is a very sensitive person with a lot of problems," his mother replied. "I'm just so sorry that I couldn't help her more. However she will be happy now that she has gone back to her home where everything is familiar and safe."

"But why did she leave?" asked Henry

"I don't know if I should tell you this, Henry, but she thought that she had seen a fully-grown elephant in the old oak tree at the bottom of the garden. She had promised that if her imagination ever took control again, she would have to go back home."

"And she isn't coming back?" asked Henry, scarcely able to control his joy. His mother shook her head sadly.

"And I can have my old room back?"

His mother could not suppress a little smile. "Yes indeed, Henry, you can have your own bedroom back. In fact even if Trixie had stayed, she wouldn't have been able to sleep in your bedroom again! This very morning she heard a tapping on the window and when she looked out she said that she saw a huge elephant looking up at her. The poor girl was terrified. I know she has made the right decision in leaving here."

Henry too felt that she had made the right decision in leaving his house, and although Ho-Ho had never met her, Ho-Ho thought so too. (Especially as it meant that he would not have to learn how to climb trees!)

The Case of Farmer Scroggins

Henry and Ho-Ho were having their morning drink of orange juice under the damson tree when Patrick the policeman arrived at the garden gate. "Hello there," he smiled. "I'm collecting old junk for a jumble sale. Henry, would you please ask your mum to leave out any old stuff she doesn't want any more and I'll collect it later." Henry was intrigued. "What is a jumbly sale?" he asked.

"Well," said Patrick, "A jumble sale is when people bring their old rubbish that they don't want any more – things like old clothes, old furniture, picture frames and the like, and other people buy it all."

"Why do they buy it if it's all rubbish?" asked Henry.

"Because," explained Patrick patiently, "Rubbish for one person may not be rubbish to another. Like if you had an old pram and the baby had grown up, or a bird cage and the bird had flown off, or a ..."

"What do you do with all of the money?" interrupted Henry.

"There's a lot of poor children around these parts," said Patrick, shaking his head. "Poor children who can't afford a holiday. With the money we make from the sale, we can take them to the seaside."

Henry thought this was a splendid idea and tried to think how he could help. "That's really nice," he finally said, "I wish we could help in some very special way for a thing like that." Ho-Ho grunted in agreement.

"I know," said Henry jumping up excitedly, "let's get Ho-Ho to give people rides on his back and charge people money for it!"

Patrick brightened. "Yes," he said, "That is a good idea!"

"And we'll go and tell everybody about the jumbly sale and get everyone to give things for it." Patrick smiled; Henry was certainly full of enthusiasm. "And the first person we will go and see is Farmer Scroggins. He has lots of rubbish. He can give us a lot of things and then his farm will look a lot tidier!"

Patrick began to laugh – just a little at first and then a great big belly laugh holding on to his big stomach. Henry looked puzzled. "Why are you laughing, Patrick? Farmer Scroggins does have lots of rubbish."

"Yes, indeed he has," said Patrick smiling and shaking his head, "But that man is a miser, Henry. He is so mean that he wouldn't even give you a piece of coal!" Henry looked quite downcast.

"I'll tell you what," continued Patrick, "If you can get Farmer Scroggins to give you anything for the jumble sale, I'll buy you a ..."

He struggled to think of something he could buy the two friends, who were already nodding at each other, as they knew what to have.

"A bucket of ice-cream!" exclaimed Henry. "A bucket of ice-cream it is!" said Patrick and the three friends all began to laugh.

Farmer Scroggins lived in a big, remote farm; in fact his only neighbours were Henry's family. He had chosen such a quiet place quite deliberately, as he was not very friendly with people at all; in fact he was very suspicious of just about everybody, thinking that they were trying to steal things from him.

As Henry and Ho-Ho climbed the hill to see him, they couldn't help but be impressed by all the things Farmer Scroggins had collected in his fields over the years. There were telephone boxes, telegraph poles, piles of tyres, a bus stop, an old mangle and even a old dentist's chair. The land was surrounded by a very impressive barbed-wire fence and Farmer Scroggins was, as usual, on patrol with his shot-gun under his arm. "Oh, it's you," he said leaning on the gate and looking from Henry to Ho-Ho, "What do you want?"

"We've just come out for a walk," said Henry, telling a little white lie, "And we thought we'd call by and say 'hello' to you."

"Hello," said Farmer Scroggins with little interest.

"We were just admiring all the things you have in your field as we came up the hill, and we were wondering where you managed to get them from?"

Farmer Scroggins stared back at Henry but didn't answer. Henry decided to carry on. "For instance, there is that wonderful old mangle. Ho-Ho and I have never seen one like that before and we wondered where you got it from. And the old dentist's chair, I've never seen one like that. It must be very valuable."

Farmer Scroggins hardly ever spoke to anyone, but he did wonder if people knew how hard he worked to collect all his valuable possessions. He had always thought that Henry was a particularly smart child. Maybe at last he had found someone to confide in. So confide he did.

For two hours Farmer Scroggins told Henry and Ho-Ho about how he had acquired all his strange 'valuable' things. They came from all over the place, from junk shops to rubbish tips and from auction houses to dustbins. Ho-Ho started snoring at one point and Henry had to gently kick him to wake him up. In fact Henry quite enjoyed the talk; when someone was very interested in what they were saying they usually made Henry interested too.

Finally it was time to go, and Henry still hadn't mentioned the jumble sale. There was no time for tact so he just asked right out if Farmer Scroggins would give some of his 'less valuable' things for the jumble sale.

Farmer Scroggins went purple. "Nobody has ever given me anything in my entire life," he declared, "So I'm certainly not going to start this giving-things-away thing now."

"But what about your friends?" asked Henry.

"Friends! Friends!" cried Farmer Scroggins, raising his voice and going an even deeper shade of purple, "What on earth would I ever want with friends?" Henry suddenly felt very sorry for the lonely old man. He felt a little tear start in his eye and reached over and touched Farmer Scroggins on his gnarled old hand. "We'll be your friends," Henry assured him, "You just see!"

It was Thursday night and Henry could not get off to sleep. On Saturday was the jumble sale and, although all was going well, Farmer Scroggins would certainly not be giving anything to help the children and Ho-Ho would not be getting the bucket of ice-cream from Patrick. And yet in a funny way, it was poor Farmer Scroggins who Henry felt most sorry for. Everyone would be at the jumble sale having fun and laughing with their friends, while poor old Farmer Scroggins would be lonely and unhappy. If only there was something he could do. Henry looked from his bedroom window in the direction of Farmer Scroggins' farm feeling very sad for the poor old man.

Then he saw it. At first he couldn't be sure, but then he was. There was a fire at Farmer Scroggins farm – definitely. Farmer Scroggins was too careful with money to have a telephone to phone for help, so a fire at his farm would be a disaster!

He quickly called out to Ho-Ho and soon the two friends were rushing in the direction of Farmer Scroggins' farm.

Farmer Scroggins was beside himself. He didn't know which way to turn. The fire was spreading towards the pile of tyres, and once they were ablaze, all of his possessions would be up in flames. In a flash Ho-Ho knew what to do; he rushed down to the well and sucked up gallons and gallons of water into his trunk. Racing back to the fire he squirted all the water out onto the flames.

It seemed to stop the fire from spreading but the fire still raged on. Ho-Ho ran down to the well for another trunk-full, and though he coughed and choked and was blackened by the smoke, he got as close to the flames as possible to put the fire out. The brave elephant charged down to the well for a third time and though the fire raged on it was only a matter of time before the sweaty, blackened and determined elephant had emptied half the well onto the flames and put the fire out.

Henry helped too of course, beating down the flames with a piece of wet carpet and shouting encouragement to the charging elephant.

The three of them sat in silence, surrounded by strange smells and smoke coming from the freshly put-out fire.

"I always pays me debts," said Farmer Scroggins. "Yes, Arthur Scroggins always pays his debts. Now, what will it be that you want?"

Among all the 'valuables' was an old ice-cream van and Ho-Ho eyed it longingly, but it had long since stopped having ice-cream in it.

"I suppose you'll be wanting me to give you some of my valuables for your jumble sale, eh?"

Somehow that didn't seem quite right to Henry; you should give things because you want to give them, not because you thought you had to.

"We really don't want anything at all," said Henry, "We just did it to help. Ho-Ho and I really enjoy helping our friends, don't we, Ho-Ho?" Henry said, turning to

Ho-Ho, who nodded with the most wonderful serious expression on his face. Hot and covered in black smoke, he did look incredibly funny.

Henry began to laugh, a happy infectious laugh. Ho-Ho joined in as usual and the two friends were soon helpless. Then came the miracle: Farmer Scroggins began to laugh too, for the first time in 35 years. It wasn't easy at first but eventually the three friends were completely out of control.

** **

The moon was full as Farmer Scroggins walked down to the gate with Henry and Ho-Ho. It had been a very strange evening. As he was about to say goodbye at the gate he said:

"Now listen, young Henry, Arthur Scroggins always pays his debts – always has and always will. You will now tell me what I have to do to make it up to you and I will. Arthur Scroggins is a man of his word!"

Henry looked at the poor old man. He just didn't know what to say. After

what seemed like an hour, he finally whispered: "What you must do is know that we are friends."

Henry and Ho-Ho turned and walked into the night, as the moon caught the slow tears shining down an old man's face.

"I really would have bought that elephant of yours a bucket of ice-cream," said Patrick, "But I knew old Scroggins would never part with a thing, so don't be too disappointed. Anyhow, everyone is really enjoying the jumble sale."

Then came the strangest sight Patrick had ever seen; it was an old farmer driving an ice-cream van, towing a cart loaded with the most amazing 'valuables' they had ever seen. To this day nobody knows how Farmer Scroggins managed to start the van, or fill it with ice-cream, or even managed to drive it down from his farm, but it certainly brought a very large cheer from the crowd. In fact it was a day for cheers; they cheered when the children rode on Ho-Ho's back, and even more so when Farmer Scroggins had a turn, but the biggest cheer of the day – and the most laughs – was when one hot and heroic elephant made an incredible mess trying to eat a bucket of ice-cream.

Henry Has Trouble with Tommy Travis

Henry and Ho-Ho were sitting under the damson tree drinking their orange juice. It was Saturday, and Henry did not go to school today. The two friends hardly needed to talk, as they often knew what the other was thinking, but today something was definitely different.

"Have you got a secret?" asked Ho-Ho.

Henry looked sad. "Well, sort of yes and sort of no," he replied.

"But if there is something worrying you, perhaps I can help?" suggested Ho-Ho. Henry remained silent for a while and then suddenly blurted out: "Have you ever been bullied, Ho-Ho?" He thought for a few moments and then added, "Of course not! Who could bully a huge elephant?"

"Yes, I have been bullied," nodded Ho-Ho encouragingly. "I really have been bullied."

Henry was fascinated to hear how a naughty mouse called Fletcher had discovered that Ho-Ho was afraid of mice and kept sneaking up on him to frighten him. He had threatened Ho-Ho and made the big elephant bring him food. Ho-Ho looked really solemn as he recalled his awful experience, and though it seemed funny to Henry that a huge creature like Ho-Ho could be scared of such a small thing like a mouse, he really did feel quite sorry for him.

"How did you get rid of Fletcher in the end?" asked Henry.

Ho-Ho thought for a moment, smiled mysteriously, and winking at Henry said: "I made friends with a cat called Sophie."

Henry was impressed that bullying could be so easily taken care of.

Sadly, that technique was certainly not going to work for his own problem.

Tommy Travis was two years older than Henry and a lot bigger and stronger. He took great delight in pushing Henry around and stealing from his lunchbox, and generally making life a misery. Henry did not know what to do; he was completely downcast.

"Perhaps we can find out what Tommy Travis is scared of?" suggested Ho-Ho. As Henry had no better ideas, it certainly seemed worth a try.

** **

That night, as soon as it was dark, Henry signalled to Ho-Ho in his tree. Ho-Ho dropped down onto the soft grass and was soon ready to go.

Tommy Travis lived about a mile from Henry on an old run-down farm, and before long the two friends were turning into the quiet lane that led to his house. They moved very quietly and slowly towards the lights ahead of them, careful not to be seen. Soon they were peeping through one of the windows and could see the Travis family – and what a sight it was! The house looked in such an awful mess and two of the windows were broken. There were five cats, as well as seven children, all crowded together in the tiny front room and everyone looked very unhappy.

"He certainly isn't scared of cats," whispered Ho-Ho.

Tommy's father was a very big man, unshaven and with his sleeves rolled up. He had grasped Tommy by the front of his shirt and was shouting very loudly at him.

"I can't trust you with anything," he yelled. "I wanted top prices for those eggs, and you bring me this!" He picked up a handful of money and threw it angrily onto the floor.

"Now you listen to me, my lad, if you don't get the money you owe me by next week, I'll give you a beating like you've never had before."

Henry and Ho-Ho were horrified; they had never seen anyone shouting quite so violently, and in spite of recent events, Henry felt quite sorry for Tommy.

"And another thing," continued the irate father, "You can stop having your light on at night. A boy of your age, frightened of the dark ... it's daft!" he spat. The look of fear on Tommy's face became much more intense.

'So Tommy is afraid of the dark,' mused Henry, finding it quite strange that a terrifying boy like Tommy could be scared of something so ordinary.

As they moved away from the house, Henry saw what he thought were giant moths flying in the moonlight. "Look at those moths!" he whispered to Ho-Ho in amazement.

"Those aren't moths," said Ho-Ho, shaking his head, "They are bats – sort of like mice that fly, except that they don't scare me as much as mice do."

Ho-Ho told Henry all about these strange flying creatures, and how they managed to fly around in the dark so fast without bumping into things. As they carried on walking they came to a huge tumbled-down barn on the edge of the Travis' farm. The bats were flying in and out of an opening high up in the roof of the barn.

"Please, Ho-Ho, give me a lift up and let me see where the bats live."

Henry was soon in an old loft, high above the floor of the barn. He could hear the Travis' hens clucking down below, but everything was in total darkness. He reached down into his pocket for his little torch. Although the battery was very weak, he could pick out these amazing flying creatures fluttering around in the gloom, and even more amazingly, hanging upside down! Henry was captivated and would have stayed for longer if Ho-Ho hadn't whispered for him to come back down. As the two friends walked home together, Henry had forgotten all about his problems with Tommy Travis. He was so excited to have discovered these magical creatures called 'bats' and he certainly wanted to go up to the loft another time when he had a proper torch.

** **

"Henry, I kept you behind the others, so I could speak to you on your own," his teacher was saying, "I know that there is something bothering you at the moment, and I think I know what it is."

Henry liked his teacher a lot and she liked Henry because he tried so hard at school. He didn't know what to say now that he knew more about Tommy Travis and how Tommy was so unhappy at home.

"I think someone might be bullying you and if they are, you must tell me. Bullies always threaten you and say they will do awful things to you if you do tell; but believe me, Henry, it is by far the best way."

Henry knew that his teacher was right; she would sort it out for him. But something was stopping him ...

"When I was a little girl, I was bullied at school and it made my life such a misery I promised that I would never let it happen to a child in my care," she continued.

His teacher was so nice trying to help him and she had been bullied too, so would understand. Henry felt confused and close to tears, he put his arms round his teacher and hugged her.

She smiled. "Are you going to tell me who it is?" she asked. Henry shook his head. "I have a very special friend and I think it will be all right," he said finally.

** **

In the playground, Tommy was looking for Henry with a new determination. He finally caught up with him and grabbed him by the collar. "I need money – and fast!" he said menacingly to Henry. He had never asked Henry for money before, but Henry remembered the threat of Tommy's father and quickly understood. Now Henry was not at all afraid; in fact he would have tried to get the money for Tommy anyway!

"Let me think," said Henry, stroking his chin in thought and puzzling Tommy by his calmness. He had some money in his money box, but if he was seen giving the money to Tommy, then Tommy would be in deep trouble and Henry did not want that to happen.

"I will have to give it to you in complete secret," he said. Tommy nodded; after all, that made sense. Henry racked his brains for somewhere secret and then remembered those amazing creatures in the barn – the bats!

"I'll meet you in the loft of your barn tonight at 10 o'clock," said Henry.

Tommy's mouth opened wide with astonishment and fear as he felt his head nodding in agreement.

Although there was a full moon, it was a cloudy night and the wind sent the clouds roaming across the sky, painting ghostly shadows across the landscape. Henry had put his money box in a big white pillowcase. The sound of him emptying his money box in the house would certainly have aroused suspicion with his mother, so he sat with Ho-Ho in the bushes by the barn counting it out.

Tommy was already terrified just being out in the dark, and the shadows made it even worse. Combining this with the faint light coming from the shrubs and what sounded like a huge animal grunting made him even more scared. He rushed into the barn and up into the loft, panting and petrified.

Finally, Henry and Ho-Ho had finished counting out the money so Ho-Ho lifted Henry up to the opening where the bats were still flying, ready to meet Tommy. Henry clutched the money, leaving the empty pillowcase with Ho-Ho. Henry seemed to appear from nowhere to the terrified Tommy, who could now scarcely even speak.

"I'm sorry I'm late," said Henry very matter-of-factly, "But I had a little bit of a hold-up." Just then there came a very strange noise indeed, as Ho-Ho began sneezing. Nobody knows why Ho-Ho started to sneeze. Perhaps it was the hens in the barn, or the mouldy straw, or perhaps some cats had been around, or maybe Ho-Ho was allergic to bats. But one thing is certain – Ho-Ho began to sneeze uncontrollably, and if you have never heard an elephant sneeze, you would be most astonished by the sound it makes.

No one knows either what Ho-Ho was trying to achieve by putting the pillowcase on the end of his trunk – most likely he was just trying to dampen the sound of the sneezes. But one thing is for sure: the sight of a pillowcase on the end of a sneezing trunk, waving past the opening in the loft would have chilled the heart of the bravest man alive, and Tommy was certainly not the bravest man alive. Henry thrust the money into Tommy's hands and the boy was gone, falling quickly down the steps of the loft and running in total terror back to the safety of his home.

"Funny," thought Henry, who had not noticed Ho-Ho waving about, "I thought he would have been pleased!"

Henry took out his torch with the new batteries and watched the bats in fascination until Ho-Ho, bored and tired, insisted they go back home.

Tommy did not appear at school for two days and when he finally did appear, he seemed quite scared of Henry. He finally plucked up courage, came up to him and gave him a brown package.

"Thanks!" said Henry, without realising that the contents of the package were in fact his money being returned. "Are you all right?" Tommy nodded – pale and speechless.

"Why did you rush off so quickly when we met in the barn?" Henry asked. At the mention of that fateful night, Tommy turned even paler, his mouth dropped open and the hairs on the back of his neck stood straight up like the prickles on a porcupine. In the blink of an eye he was gone.

"That's a pity," thought Henry, "I wanted to tell him all about the bats."

"Yes," said Henry's teacher to the headmaster, "I was very worried about Henry. I was convinced that he was being bullied by Tommy Travis, but I have been watching them carefully and now Tommy seems to be actually avoiding Henry. In fact the only time I did see them together Tommy gave Henry a present. Anyhow, Henry seems back to his old self, so the matter is now closed. I'm giving some more attention to Tommy though, as I think he and his family might need some more help. Tommy is certainly a very vulnerable child."

The headmaster nodded in agreement; the matter of Henry was certainly now closed, and Henry was certainly his old happy and resourceful self.

For his own part, Henry didn't even know what 'resourceful' meant; he just knew that things tend to work out if you try hard and trust yourself. Tommy obviously had a lot more problems than Henry did, and Henry actually ended up feeling rather sorry for him. In fact one day in the future he would even help Tommy overcome his fear of the dark, but that is another story.

Author's Note: Many children suffer from being bullied and maybe just knowing that the bully is probably also quite vulnerable just might be helpful to the bullied child!

Ho-Ho's Tree Under Threat

Not all of Henry's life was fun and adventure – not by a long way. He had his own set of jobs to do around the house and the garden, and sometimes he had to sit and meet some of his mother's friends and 'be on his best behaviour', which could be terribly boring.

The jobs in the garden and greenhouse were nice really – they just took a lot of time. Henry liked watching plants grow and change, caring for them as they burst into bud and then flowered. His favourite flower was called a 'white lapageria' – a beautiful greenhouse flower that his Uncle Elgar had given him. Uncle Elgar had a most unusual passion for the white lapageria and had somehow passed on his enthusiasm to Henry, who had looked after it very, very carefully indeed. He had taken lots of cuttings and now had a fine collection of white lapagerias. He would have loved to show Uncle Elgar his collection, but his mother and Uncle Elgar had fallen out and hadn't spoken to each other for about three years.

Today, however, it was 'best behaviour' day as the vicar and Miss Didcott had called in for 'afternoon tea'. They went through the usual routines of saying how big Henry was getting and asked about his school and 'what a clever boy he was', (Henry knew the lines by heart), and then settled in to that boring chatter that made Henry very sleepy indeed. Though he smiled and tried to look interested, his mind was elsewhere – at the seaside with Ho-Ho, re-living some of their adventures together and dreaming up new ones.

"Yes indeed," the vicar was saying between buttered scones, 'The Dawsons have got the most beautiful front lawn, made nicer, methinks, by that wonderful pagoda."

'Perhaps if a thunder-and-lightning storm started, they might go home,' wondered Henry to himself.

"Lawns take a lot of care to be in prime condition," the vicar continued, "A lot of care and a lot of planning. Don't you agree Miss Didcott?" Miss Didcott did of course agree.

"Perhaps if I really concentrated, I could make myself come out in spots and then they'd have to go home," wondered Henry.

"Lawns are so extremely English," continued the vicar, "We almost have a national duty to them." He smiled at his own wit and the ladies smiled too.

"... Or if a swarm of bees flew into the house, they might leave," Henry's thoughts continued, making him smile at the prospect of the grown-ups being chased by a swarm of bees.

"Ah," said the vicar, noticing the smile, "I see you appreciate humour, Henry." Henry nodded.

"If I hadn't been a vicar," he droned on, "I could have been a garden designer. I sometimes feel that one is closer to God when working with nature." The ladies nodded at the vicar's wisdom.

"... Or perhaps if a mouse ran out from under the settee," mused Henry smiling to himself again.

"I see that amuses you too, Henry – the idea of your dear vicar becoming a mere gardener, but let me tell you, I've often thought about it. For instance, your own front lawn with that unsightly damson tree right in the middle; if I were you," he said turning to Henry's mother, "I would dig the old tree out and replace it with ..." he looked up, trying to picture the ideal replacement, "A small lily pond – with goldfish!" He nodded, convinced that his wisdom had more than paid for the tea and scones he had just eaten.

Henry woke up at this last idea. "Mummy, I really, really love that damson tree, p-p-please don't even think about hurting it."

"Don't be silly, dear," said Henry's mother, "The vicar is quite right, and certainly if the old tree doesn't flower in the next few weeks, it will have to go."

Henry was horrified and in spite of his mother's instructions, rushed out of the room with tears in his eyes.

"Children these days," said the vicar shaking his head. "Now when I was a boy ..."

Later, under the damson tree, Henry explained to Ho-Ho about the threat to have their very own tree removed. The situation was very serious indeed.

"Whatever can we do, Ho-Ho?" said Henry, very upset. "If the damson tree doesn't flower, they are going to cut it down."

Ho-Ho looked very wise. "This is a tree problem," he said at last, "Definitely a tree problem."

Henry looked at Ho-Ho with disappointment. Of course it was a tree problem. Strange that Ho-Ho, who knew just about everything, said such simple and obvious things. Then an idea struck him: "Ho-Ho, the very best person for tree problems is my Uncle Elgar; we must go and see him!" Henry clapped his hands with delight; if it was a problem to do with flowers or trees, Uncle Elgar was the finest man for the job.

** **

Henry ran almost all the way to Uncle Elgar's cottage, though it was nearly two miles from his own house.

Uncle Elgar was hoeing round some roses, but looked up and smiled as Henry came hurtling down the path.

He was very fond of his nephew, and was only sorry that a silly family quarrel with Henry's mother had kept them from seeing each other more often.

"Now calm down and tell me all about it, but very slowly, please! Even your Uncle Elgar can't make a damson tree flower overnight!"

Henry explained slowly about the vicar and his theories about lawns and the damson tree.

Uncle Elgar shook his head. He truly couldn't understand why Henry was so upset about an old tree. However, if it was important to Henry, then he would do his best to put things right. But how could he go and inspect the tree without meeting Henry's mother? His mind drifted back to the argument that had led to the fall-out between them.

"You see, Henry, I was the judge of a flower show and your mother – my sister – had a very beautiful entry. I can still remember it to this day, it was so beautiful, wonderful white lilies contrasting with blood-red roses. But the title of the section was 'Unusual beauties in unusual combinations' and that is what your mother did not understand. Of course, everyone thought her entry was by far the most beautiful, but Anthea Robotham's 'Lapagerias and bluebells' was far more unusual. I really had no choice but to give Anthea the prize."

A few things Henry had overheard now made sense, such as his mother calling Anthea 'Elgar's girlfriend'. She had thought that Elgar had shown favouritism at the show.

"Is Anthea your girlfriend?" asked Henry innocently. Elgar burst into a loud and very genuine laugh, "Henry, Henry, Henry," he said, shaking his head and going quite thoughtful. "This is my girlfriend," he said, waving his hand at all the beautiful flowers and shrubs surrounding his cottage, "And this is my real true love," he said, picking a white lapageria and holding it close to his tender gaze.

** **

It had all been carefully arranged. On Wednesdays Henry's mother went shopping in the city and Henry had called on Uncle Elgar to let him know that the coast was clear. They drove round to Henry's house in Uncle Elgar's battered old van, loaded with garden tools and materials. (Elgar often did gardening jobs for extra money.)

"Hmmmm," said Elgar looking up into the branches of the damson tree and stroking his chin, "Very interesting indeed." He picked up a spade and turned over a piece of earth at the base of the tree, picked up a handful of soil, crumbling it between his fingers and sniffing.

"Yes indeed, Henry," he announced, looking very wise indeed, "Uncle Elgar knows where the trouble lies. You see, Henry, soil is living stuff, full of tiny creatures and thousands and thousands of minerals – and humus." He was trying to impress Henry with his knowledge, but there was no need whatsoever as Henry was always totally in awe of Uncle Elgar's knowledge.

"And this tree," he continued, gesturing to the damson tree, "Is suffering from a deficiency – a shortage – of a mineral called magnesium!"

"But can you mend it?" Henry asked, a note of desperation in his voice. Elgar folded his arms and looked up for a minute. "Of course I can!" he winked teasingly at Henry, "Would your Uncle Elgar let you down?"

Henry helped Uncle Elgar to bring some Epsom salts, which contained the magnesium the tree needed, from his van. They dug some shallow holes in several places around the tree and put two handfuls of the salts into each hole, finally covering them over as before.

"And that," announced Elgar, "Is the problem solved; your tree will flower as normal in about four weeks. It already has buds on it, it was just the shortage of magnesium that stopped them from growing into flowers. Now, Henry, show me around the garden."

It was a delight for Henry to show his wonderful uncle around the garden, for Uncle Elgar seemed to know everything about every single plant – whether each plant liked shade or sun, how often they should be watered and fed; he was an absolute font of knowledge.

They finally came to the greenhouse where the white lapagerias looked even more beautiful than normal, as though they knew that today they should put on a special show. Uncle Elgar was speechless. His face changed colour and he had to sit down. There were tears in his eyes as he shook his head.

"My lovely sister. My poor dear little sister," he whispered quietly to himself.

Things moved on nicely after that. First a big van drew up to Henry's house and a man in a uniform handed over a bunch of beautiful flowers to Henry's mother. It was the biggest bunch of lilies and red roses that Henry had ever seen. When she read the note attached to them, Henry's mother seemed very deeply moved.

Then came the miracle: the damson tree burst into flower and Henry burst into the house to tell his mother the good news. He was breathless with excitement and accidentally let slip about the help he had received from Uncle Elgar. He realised his mistake too late, but there was no turning back now. Defiantly he said, "Uncle Elgar is truly wonderful and I love him!"

"So do I," said his mother quietly and then, almost as if it had been deliberately timed, there was a knock on the front door. Soon Henry was slipping out of the back door, leaving brother and sister in a tearful embrace.

Henry and Ho-Ho sat under the flowering damson tree drinking their orange juice. "... So you see, Ho-Ho, all the damson tree needed was some magneesijump," Henry finished importantly, getting his words wrong as usual. Ho-Ho nodded. "One thing does puzzle me though, Ho-Ho," he said, looking at his friend quizzically, "You are the cleverest and wisest friend in the whole world, so you must have known what was wrong from the very start."

Ho-Ho nodded matter-of-factly.

"So why didn't you tell me when I first asked?"

Ho-Ho thought for a while. "Sometimes things seem broken and impossible when the answer is very simple," said Ho-Ho, stating the obvious as usual, "You needed the right answer ... from the right person ... at the right time."

Henry thought about his mother, Uncle Elgar, the lapagerias, the roses, the lilies and the damson tree, and understood in a strange, deep way that his friend was right.

"Besides," Ho-Ho went on, "Whoever would have believed an elephant?!"

The two friends laughed until the tears rolled down their cheeks.

A Very Mysterious Illness

Henry's mother looked most concerned. She shook her head as she looked at Henry. "You'll have to stay right here in bed today," she said. "I've spoken to Dr Munro and he says that all the children in the village are sick with this flu."

"What's flu?" asked Henry in a very weak voice, for he certainly didn't feel like going anywhere.

"Well," said his mother, looking up at the ceiling, "It's when germs get into your body and attack your insides and make you feel ill." Henry was none the wiser, though he certainly did feel rather ill and so was pretty sure that his mother was right.

"When I had the flu," continued his mother, "My grandmother used to give me mustard seeds and orange drinks to get me better." She pointed to the big jug of orange juice and a jar of mustard seeds by its side. Henry's mother was a great believer in her grandmother's cures, though no one else seemed to have much faith in them.

"By the way, Henry, I don't suppose you know of someone called Ho-Ho, do you?" Henry gulped; somehow it would be terrible if his mother found out about his friend Ho-Ho the elephant. "You see, Henry, there is a strange parcel downstairs addressed to him, with your name on it too. It looks like one of Uncle Dennis's old tricks, if you ask me!"

"Please let me see it," begged Henry, "I'll get it to him somehow." Any mention of Uncle Dennis brought Henry to full attention. Uncle Dennis always seemed to be doing exciting things and somehow protecting Henry from a long way away.

"All right," smiled Henry's mother, kissing him on the forehead, "You won't be doing anything else today." Henry heard her walk downstairs. This was most mysterious, for Uncle Dennis rarely wrote to Henry without a very special reason, and he had never written to Ho-Ho. In fact Henry had never even met the mysterious Uncle Dennis, though he often thought about him and prayed that they would meet one day. "Here it is," she said at last, putting a very strange parcel on Henry's bed.

"Now do try to get some sleep, drink plenty of orange juice and swallow some of the mustard seeds. I'll try not to disturb you. Just bang hard on the floor if you need anything."

The door closed behind her, leaving Henry staring at the parcel. It was about the size of a small cushion, very carefully wrapped with strange, blue, thick string and the stamps were most peculiar, from a country that Henry had never heard of. Uncle Dennis was always full of surprises!

Henry must have dozed off to sleep, for the next thing he noticed was the tap, tap, tapping on the window. It was Ho-Ho tapping with his trunk.

"Ho-Ho, I can't come out today because I've got the froop." (Henry had got his words wrong again!) Ho-Ho looked puzzled and Henry couldn't help smiling.

"What's the froop?" asked Ho-Ho.

Henry tried to look grown-up, "It's sort of little things that get inside your body and bite. They make you hot and shiver and feel bad so you have to take mustard and orange."

"What sort of little things?" asked Ho-Ho.

"Well, sort of worms," said Henry trying to sound confident, but then remembering what elephants were really frightened of, "A bit like mice, but very, very tiny so they can live inside your body."

"That sounds terrible," said Ho-Ho shaking his head and looking very sorry for his little friend, "Why doesn't your body get rid of them?"

"It just sort of takes a bit of time," said Henry, "You get the mice, then your body gets them to leave and then you get better."

"Yes," said Ho-Ho, nodding wisely. Suddenly he noticed the parcel on Henry's bed. "Whatever is that?" he asked.

"It's a present for you from Uncle Dennis," said Henry brightening, "Shall we open it?"

Henry carefully slipped off the blue string; there were three layers of thick brown paper and then inside was a red box. Clearly written on it in big letters was the message: "Only to be opened outside."

The two friends looked at each other. Really Henry should have stayed indoors, but this was a special present from Uncle Dennis, and, well, things always turned out all right when Uncle Dennis was involved. The two friends nodded in agreement. In the blink of an eye, Henry had clambered down Ho-Ho's trunk and was on the lawn underneath the damson tree, where they took the lid off the red box. Inside were a red balloon and a red envelope. Henry opened the envelope. It was one of those strange rhymes from Uncle Dennis:

> Let the box lie under the tree,
> The balloon lies on the lid you see,
> Let your eye-lids close right over your eyes,
> Dream your dreams and off to the skies!

"Right," said Henry, "Help me back into my bedroom." He went back to the house, climbed up Ho-Ho's trunk and put the empty box under the bed covers, which made it look as though Henry was still lying there. "Oh, and I mustn't forget the mustard seeds and the orange," thought Henry, remembering his mother's instructions.

Back under the damson tree, they put the balloon on top of the lid, and sat and watched; nothing happened. "Now we must close our eyes," said Henry.

They closed their eyes. At first all was silent, then Henry noticed a strange sound, faint at first, like air rushing out of a punctured tyre and he began to feel a little dizzy, almost as if he was floating. "I think it is time to open our eyes now, Ho-Ho. Let's open our eyes together. I'll count to three and on the count of three, we will open them. One ... two ... three!"

The two friends opened their eyes, and then opened them even wider with total amazement. They could not believe what they were seeing, for they were floating high up in the air. The small balloon had become enormous and they were both sitting in the lid of the box, which was dangling underneath the balloon. Henry could just about recognise his house, which had become quite small from such a distance. For a while the two friends were speechless, just enjoying a wonderful feeling of floating so high up, like being lost in a beautiful dream. "We must always trust Uncle Dennis," said Henry. Ho-Ho nodded; things certainly did seem to work well when they did trust him. As the balloon floated higher and higher, there seemed no need to talk. It was as if ideas came into their minds at the same time. They were just wondering, drifting and dreaming, and trusting what Uncle Dennis had got planned for them. The balloon seemed to know where it was going, just as Henry's body seemed to know how to cure itself. It was just a matter of trusting, and watching and waiting for things to happen.

It seemed they drifted for days, but the sun hadn't stopped shining so it must have only been hours or even just minutes; time seemed so unimportant. Then the balloon began to slowly drop down. Henry became a little worried as they were obviously floating over the sea, but soon a beautiful island came into view. They were going to land on a beautiful island!

The balloon slowly drifted onto a wonderful golden beach and gently settled into the soft sand. This was indeed a beautiful island: the sea was so blue and the golden sands stretched as far as the eye could see. In the distance were some small boats and Henry thought he could see some fishing nets being pulled in. Up on the island, the trees were green; the whole place seemed like the way his mother had described Heaven to him. Presently he noticed four small children running towards them. They were happy, and obviously quite excited, pointing at Henry and Ho-Ho.

"Where are we?" Henry asked the children.

The children giggled.

"Do you know where we are?" asked Henry again.

A little girl stepped forward. "This is called Harmony Island," she said, smiling and waving her hand at the beautiful scenery. "And who are you?" she asked.

"I am called Henry, and this is my friend Ho-Ho the elephant," said Henry, trying to sound confident.

"You must be very hungry," said the little girl, looking concerned. "Come with us and we'll see if we can find some food."

Henry and Ho-Ho were feeling very hungry. They stepped out of the balloon and followed the children. When the children heard about their amazing journey in the balloon, they were most impressed and wanted to know everything about

Uncle Dennis, Ho-Ho and all the adventures that had happened to the two friends.

"Perhaps you have been sent to help us," said a very little, thin boy with big, wide eyes. Henry couldn't help smiling; after all, how could these children possibly need help, living as they did on this beautiful island? They stopped to rest under a huge tree.

"Did you come all this way without any food?" asked the little girl.

"I've got some orange and mustard seeds," said Henry, producing the jug of orange juice and the jar of mustard seeds. The children tasted the orange juice and thought it was beautiful; when they tasted the mustard seeds, however, there were yelps of horror – they couldn't believe that anything could taste so horrible! Henry and Ho-Ho couldn't help laughing at the expressions on the children's faces when they tasted the mustard seeds.

"Why would anyone eat that?" asked the little girl.

"It's because Henry has got mice," said Ho-Ho wisely. The children were suddenly shocked. All their eyes fixed on Henry in total horror.

Henry was rather embarrassed. "Well," he said, "It's more that I've got the froop, and little things like mice get inside your body and bite your insides, making you hot and feel sick. And then your body finds a way to scare them away and you get better."

Since he had been in the balloon, Henry had begun feeling so much better. His mother was always right about these things, but perhaps in that magic balloon his body had been learning quickly how to scare off these 'mice' inside his body.

Meanwhile, Ho-Ho had become very hungry and reached up into the big tree with his trunk, pulling down a huge bunch of bananas, which he shared with the children. The children were obviously very hungry and Henry couldn't help noticing how thin they were. They were absolutely thrilled with the bananas and the amazing elephant who could reach so high up into the tree. Even as they were eating, they seemed quite nervous, continually looking around as though they expected something bad to happen. Ho-Ho pulled down lots more bananas until they were all full up.

"That was wonderful," said the girl, with total amazement in her voice. "You see, Ho-Ho, we can never eat our food in peace because of the mice." The other children nodded. "Our island is overrun with these strange mice that eat all our food. There is a lot of food on the island, but the mice eat it all and that's why we are always hungry."

So that was it. Now Henry understood the looks of horror when Ho-Ho had explained about the froop and his mice. He felt very sad that the mice had stopped the people of the island from being happy. But why had the mice stayed away when all the children were enjoying Ho-Ho's bananas? As if she had been reading his mind, the girl clapped her hands and jumped up.

"The mice are frightened of you," she explained. "If you will stay with us and guard our food, the mice will leave us alone. Please, please stay with us for ever on the island."

Henry and Ho-Ho looked at each other. They certainly wanted to help the children, but even though the island was like Heaven, they didn't want to stay trapped there forever, as they had lots of things to do and lots of friends they would like to see again.

They decided to go for a walk over the island and think it over. The children were talking excitedly together as Henry and Ho-Ho disappeared into the forest. They walked for miles and miles in deep thought.

"What can we do?" said Henry with tears in his eyes. "We can't leave these poor children to the mice, but we can't stay trapped here forever either." The very thought of not seeing his friends and his home again made Henry very sad indeed.

"Uncle Dennis wouldn't send you to prison," said Ho-Ho with a confident laugh, "There must be some other way." Henry knew that his wise old friend was right.

The two friends sat down and Henry carelessly peeled the banana he had brought with him, took a bite and put it down on the floor, deep in thought. Suddenly there was a rustling in the bushes and as they looked up, dozens of strange-looking mice appeared. They were nothing like the mice that Henry had ever seen before. They were a strange orange colour with pink whiskers and yellow teeth.

Ho-Ho was terrified, lifted Henry onto his back and sped off in the direction they had come, leaving the mice greedily eating the banana.

They finally stopped for Ho-Ho to get his breath back.

"We can't leave the children to those mice," said Henry, "They are horrible!"

"But I'm scared of them," said Ho-Ho, "And they certainly don't seem very scared of me." In a flash Henry had the answer: the mice had come for Henry's banana, so it obviously wasn't Ho-Ho that scared them. There was only one answer ... it was the mustard seeds!

** **

By the time Henry and Ho-Ho had returned to the children, the whole village was there. Everyone seemed very happy around the big campfire, with the smell of fish cooking and no sign of the mice. As Henry and Ho-Ho came out of the bushes, everyone began to clap and cheer. Finally they all sat down on the grass and the little girl asked Henry what they had decided to do, begging the two friends to stay on the island forever. Henry told them all about the experience of the mice stealing his banana and how they weren't at all afraid of Henry or of Ho-Ho. When he told them how frightened Ho-Ho had been of the little mice, they all laughed at such a ridiculous idea of a big elephant being scared of such tiny creatures. Ho-Ho blushed, but joined in the laughter. Henry then explained that it was the smell of the mustard seeds that kept the mice away. The children nodded; having tasted mustard, they could certainly understand why!

There was a murmur as the people discussed Henry's story. Finally the little girl stood up. "What we must do," she said, picking up the jar of mustard seeds, "Is to plant these seeds all over the island and then we will be safe from the mice. The island will belong to our people again."

The people cheered and, after the meeting, immediately set to work planting the seeds all over the island.

And that is exactly how Henry and Ho-Ho saved Harmony Island from the mice. As they floated off in the balloon, Henry was sure he could see thousands of tiny mice racing down to the beach and swimming into the sea where they would be safe from the mustard. Then gradually the whole island disappeared into the distance and just the feeling of peace, dreaming, drifting and feeling good remained.

He dreamt about the island and the mice; it almost seemed as if his body had been cleared of his mice, just like on the island where they had been driven off into the sea. He looked at his best friend Ho-Ho and knew that between them they could solve almost any problem. He didn't know whether he was asleep or awake as he drifted in the magic balloon, but he did know that things happen for the best.

Sure enough, the balloon brought them back to the safety of their own garden and, as he climbed in through his bedroom window, it looked as though he was still asleep in bed, but of course, it was the box he had put under the sheets. Then he drifted off into a very deep sleep, totally exhausted by his adventures.

Henry's mother was drawing the curtains in his bedroom.

"It is really amazing how quickly you have got better," she said. "Every time I looked in yesterday you were fast asleep, so I didn't disturb you. It must have been the mustard seeds that made you better! What I don't understand is whatever happened to the jar and the jug of orange juice!"

Henry smiled. He knew where they were, and he knew there was a place where he would always be welcome, where Ho-Ho and Henry could go whenever they wanted and if ever they needed help ... they could go to Harmony Island!

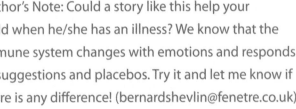

Author's Note: Could a story like this help your child when he/she has an illness? We know that the immune system changes with emotions and responds to suggestions and placebos. Try it and let me know if there is any difference! (bernardshevlin@fenetre.co.uk)

Ho-Ho Learns to Sing

"Now listen carefully, Henry," said his mother looking very serious, "I have to be away for the whole day to visit my sister, and I really don't like to leave you on your own."

"Please don't worry about me, mummy, I'll be just fine!" said Henry, who really didn't want to 'go visiting' people and miss all the fun of being with Ho-Ho. The journeys tended to be very tedious and he always had to be on his 'best behaviour', which could be very tiring indeed! His mother was quite aware of Henry's preferences and, rather than drag a tired and rather grumpy little boy around, accepted that he had best stay at home on his own. However, she had prepared a huge picnic basket to last him through the day.

"Now if there are any problems whatsoever, you can always telephone Uncle Elgar, who is not far away and will come straight round."

Of course, Henry's mother did not know about Ho-Ho, and if she had known, she would have felt very happy about him being in such safe company.

** **

Later, under the damson tree, Henry was explaining to Ho-Ho why they had such a huge picnic basket and how his mother had left him at home alone.

"Do you get frightened when your mummy leaves you?" asked Ho-Ho.

"Not when you are here!" said Henry.

"What do you do when you do get frightened?" asked Ho-Ho.

"Hmmm," thought Henry for a moment, "I think I usually sing," he finally added.

"What is singing?" asked Ho-Ho, looking puzzled.

Henry was at a loss to explain what singing is to an elephant, so instead he began to sing, to show him. He started with 'Twinkle, Twinkle, Little Star' and then went through all the songs he knew, even the ones about Christmas. All the time, Ho-Ho looked fascinated and full of admiration.

"That is wonderful!" exclaimed Ho-Ho. "Do you think I will be able to sing?" Henry thought for a moment, because he had never heard of an elephant singing.

"I'm sure you will be able to, if you practise," he said finally.

So Ho-Ho began to practise singing. The noise was deafening, but the expression on Ho-Ho's face of complete concentration and determination to master the art of singing made Henry laugh. He laughed so much that there were tears rolling down his cheeks.

In the future, when they looked back on that day, Henry and Ho-Ho would always remember it as their 'musical festival'. They spent the whole afternoon singing, drinking orange juice and eating from the picnic basket. It was a wonderful and very funny day they spent together.

The next day, Mr Crabbitt came round. Mr Crabbitt didn't particularly like Henry; in fact Mr Crabbitt didn't particularly like anybody. When Henry heard the important knock on the door and realised that it was Mr Crabbitt, he knew there must be trouble of some sort. He went downstairs to find out.

"The noise was just deafening, and definitely coming from your property," Mr Crabbitt was complaining to Henry's mother, who listened very patiently indeed.

"Henry, do you have any ideas about this noise that Mr Crabbitt is talking about?" she asked him.

Henry felt very flustered and was most anxious that the grown-ups should not realise the truth – that it had been an elephant learning to sing making all the noise yesterday afternoon!

"I was singing in a very loud voice," said Henry.

"Humph," said Mr Crabbitt. "It was more like a, a, a ..." – he searched for the right description. "An elephant!" he finally announced.

Henry's mother promised to look into this mystery and Henry secretly decided that he must warn Ho-Ho that his singing practices must stop!

Under the damson tree later that morning, Henry and Ho-Ho were discussing Mr Crabbitt.

"He really is a very unhappy man," said Henry, "It would be very nice to make friends with him. Do you have any ideas, Ho-Ho?"

Ho-Ho scratched his chin with his trunk, and looked very wise indeed.

"Some people only make friends when they really need someone," he finally said.

Henry thought for a minute. "That's it!" he finally said, "We just have to find out what Mr Crabbitt needs, solve his problem and then we will be his friends!"

Henry and Ho-Ho decided to call round to Mr Crabbitt's house and find out any problems he might have. They pressed on Ho-Ho's magic button so that he became very small and, with Ho-Ho in his pocket, Henry walked round to his neighbour's property.

There was a public footpath that went through the land belonging to Mr Crabbitt. It was the law that anyone was allowed to use this footpath, but Mr Crabbitt was always very suspicious of people and was continually watching to make sure that they did no damage and didn't stray from the path. Not surprisingly, he was there waiting when the two friends arrived.

"Stick to the path and make sure that you close all the farm gates; I don't want my animals escaping!" he said in a very grumpy voice. Then he noticed that it was Henry.

"Oh, it's you, is it? Young Master Henry."

"Hello again, Mr Crabbitt, what beautiful cows you have," said Henry brightly, "And what a beautiful field. What are those lovely yellow flowers?"

"Those are called cowslips," replied Mr Crabbitt reluctantly, "And as for a beautiful field, can you not see, young man, all those molehills?"

"What are molehills?" asked Henry. Mr Crabbitt explained about these small creatures called moles, which live under the ground and dig tunnels, depositing the earth in mounds called molehills. Henry could see lots and lots of molehills and quickly realised he had found something that Mr Crabbitt needed. Mr Crabbitt was very unhappy about this 'invasion' of his land by these creatures and though he had called in many experts, nobody had been able to shift the moles from his land. Henry listened in total fascination and the old farmer even began to melt a little at someone who seemed sympathetic to his plight.

Henry was fascinated by the small creatures who spent all their days tunnelling under the earth and scooping it out, living on worms and tiny creatures under the soil, but then he remembered his mission.

"Shall I try to get rid of the moles?" Henry asked innocently.

The old farmer melted a little more but began to laugh. "I've called in all the experts and they just took my money and did no good whatsoever. If you could get rid of those moles, I would be very grateful and I would give you ...." As the farmer tried to think of a suitable gift, Henry remembered that Ho-Ho was in his pocket and came to his assistance.

"A bucket of ice-cream?"

"It's a deal!" said the old farmer, shaking Henry's hand and smiling for the first time that year.

Henry finally found a quiet spot where he could not be seen and Ho-Ho became his full size. The two friends discussed the problem.

"How can we get those moles to leave Mr Crabbitt's fields?" asked Henry. Ho-Ho thought for a long time.

"We ought to go down into the tunnels they make and see for ourselves what they do," said Ho-Ho. The two friends agreed that Ho-Ho would shrink down to his smallest size and crawl down into one of the tunnels. They were all apparently connected together, so he would be able to get a good idea of what the moles did and how to persuade them to leave the area. Henry got his little spade and began digging into a molehill until he found the tunnel. Ho-Ho shrunk down to his smallest size and Henry dropped him into the tunnel. Then he waited and waited and waited ...

** **

It seemed like hours that Ho-Ho had been gone and Henry was beginning to worry about his friend, when suddenly, a little distance away from Henry, there seemed to be an earthquake starting. The land shook, and a little hill appeared, which got bigger and bigger and then began to shake. Henry was quite scared, wondering what it could be, when Ho-Ho's trunk appeared from the middle of the shaking earth. Then slowly – a little bit at a time – the earth shook some more and then dropped away to reveal his friend Ho-Ho, smiling and looking very pleased with himself indeed.

"I've just had an adventure all by myself!" said Ho-Ho. The two friends sat down and Ho-Ho told the story of his adventures down the mole tunnels.

Apparently he had walked quite a distance before he came across the first mole, and the creature had looked so fierce, with big sharp teeth and big claws, that

Ho-Ho had run away at first. Eventually he had turned and faced the fierce little creature, which looked as though it wanted to eat Ho-Ho. Worse was to come as more and more moles had come to help and find out who this stranger was that had invaded their tunnels. For a moment it had looked as though all the moles of the field were together in a gang ready to attack Ho-Ho.

Henry was fascinated by the story. "Whatever did you do, Ho-Ho?" he asked.

"Well," said Ho-Ho, looking very wise and thoughtful, "I was very frightened and I remembered that you had told me that when you were frightened you like to sing, so I just started singing!" Even though he was very tiny, the sound of Ho-Ho singing was pretty scary and in the small space of the tunnels it must have been terrifying! The poor creatures had run away in a total panic as quickly as their little legs would take them! The way Ho-Ho had described the incident, Henry was sure that the problem had been resolved, and he felt so proud that it was his friend who had fixed the problem for good.

Later that day, Henry knocked on Mr Crabbitt's door. "I think I've got your moles to leave," said Henry as soon as Mr Crabbitt answered it. Mr Crabbitt looked very doubtful indeed. He knew that the only way that you can tell that the moles have gone is if new molehills stop appearing and that would take a few days to find out.

"So Master Henry, how did you manage to get the moles to leave?" he said, not believing Henry one bit, but fascinated by the little boy's efforts to help his plight. Henry thought for moment as he dare not reveal the truth, but did not want to tell a complete lie. "I sort of had to do some digging and then sort of organised some special singing," he added.

Mr Crabbitt smiled for the second time that year. "Oh yes, your singing ... the noise that disturbed all my cows the other day! Well, if you have got those moles to move away, I will bring you that bucket of ice-cream I promised."

They shook hands and bade farewell. Mr Crabbitt saw the fields where Henry and Ho-Ho had been and was very impressed by Henry's so-called 'digging', which was in fact the place where Ho-Ho had emerged from the tunnels.

A week passed by. Henry was just about to go outside to meet Ho-Ho under the damson tree with a drink of orange juice when there was a knock at the door.

"Ah, Mr Crabbitt," said Henry's mother a little apprehensively, "And what have you got there?"

"It is a bucket of ice-cream for young Master Henry. He is a very clever little boy who has got rid of the moles from my fields."

Mr Crabbitt seemed very friendly, and sat down and had a cup of tea with Henry's mother, discussing life on the farm and how the countryside was blooming at this time of the year. Henry excused himself, as he was very anxious to get out to Ho-Ho and tell him the good news.

"Henry is a wonderful little boy," said Mr Crabbitt, "He is very clever – especially at getting rid of moles! And don't worry about the noise the other day, Henry's singing is something to be very proud of, and if he needs to practise, I will certainly put up with the noise!"

Henry's mother looked absolutely astonished and could not really understand what the farmer was trying to say. Not that it mattered; it was just so nice to see her neighbour so much more happy and friendly. They remained friends for a long time afterwards.

And it certainly didn't matter to a certain elephant and a little boy who were enjoying a bucket of ice-cream together and making such a mess that normally would have led to Henry being scolded. But some days turn out so well that small things like ice-cream messes don't really matter at all!

Ho-Ho Goes Missing

One morning when Henry woke up, the sun was shining through his bedroom window and the sky was a beautiful blue, but something felt wrong. For a while he lay there staring at the ceiling trying to think what it could be, then it struck him. "Shouldn't Ho-Ho be here by now?" he wondered. He went downstairs where his mother was making some coffee.

"You're late this morning, Henry," she said. "Would you like some breakfast?"

"No thanks," said Henry, "Just a very big glass of orange juice please. I'll drink it under the damson tree."

Henry went out with his huge glass of orange juice and sat under the tree, where he waited. And waited. And waited. But nothing happened. Or rather, a certain elephant did not appear. "Ho-Ho," Henry whispered loudly up into the tree, "Ho-Ho, come on down." He peered up into the branches, but there was no sign of any movement, and no sign at all of a tiny pink elephant, hanging upside down.

Then he smelt it – the smell of freshly mown grass. The lawns had been cut with a motor-mower! Henry panicked; what if Ho-Ho had come down from his tree and been torn to bits by the lawnmower before he became his full size? Henry was in a panic. He ran into the house.

"Mummy! Mummy! Have you mowed the lawn? Where have you put the cut grass?" he cried out.

"Henry, do calm down," said his mother. "I can't imagine why you want to know, but it is on the compost heap in the usual place."

Henry dashed out of the house to the compost heap and began looking through

the grass cuttings, expecting at any moment to find the damaged body of his friend Ho-Ho. He must have gone through every single blade of grass in the compost heap at least three times but there was no sign of Ho-Ho.

He dashed back to the damson tree and shouted up into its branches. "Ho-Ho, Ho-Ho! Come on down, please, Ho-Ho?"

Henry kept calling until he couldn't shout any more. Finally he just sat down and cried. The tears ran down his cheeks and onto the lawn. He cried as he hadn't cried since he was a baby. He cried the burning tears of someone who had lost their dearest friend.

Finally he stopped, and stared sadly at the tree.

"Oh Ho-Ho, where can you be?" he whispered in despair. "If only you were here, we would know what to do," he thought out loud.

It seemed such a long time since he had been forced to think completely on his own, without Ho-Ho's help.

Suddenly he had an idea; he decided to pretend that Ho-Ho was really there and to imagine what he would say. As hard as he could, he imagined himself saying, "Ho-Ho, I can't find Ho-Ho and I want to find him more than anything else in the world. Where should I look?" Henry thought back to the times they had sat together trying to solve a problem. He pictured Ho-Ho's wise old face, thinking and then saying something really simple, which time after time had led to the answer. Then he heard in his mind the voice of Ho-Ho saying, "Well, Henry, he does live up a tree."

"That's it!" thought Henry, "He must still be up his tree! Perhaps he got stuck or something! That must be the answer!"

Henry dashed over to the tree. His mother had told him never to climb the damson tree as the branches were quite slippery and not very strong even for Henry's weight. But this was an emergency and Henry was a very good climber. The damson tree was even more dangerous and slippery than usual and Henry knew he had to be very, very careful indeed. He very cautiously climbed the bottom branches and then felt confident enough to try the higher, more dangerous part. "Ho-Ho!" he whispered loudly as he started the climb. Then the tears came gushing uncontrollably once again and everything went black.

There were sirens and people shouting and saying strange things like, "Is he still breathing?" His mother was beside herself, crying.

"My little boy, will he be all right? I told him never to climb that tree, please save him!" Then there was a bumpy journey in an ambulance and so many people trying to help. There was a mask over his face to help his breathing and a really bad pain in his head. But none of it mattered to Henry; all he wanted was to see his friend again.

When they arrived at the hospital he was moved onto some kind of trolley and taken to a very safe ward where they could watch over him and treat him. Then came the tears and the blackness once again; he just wanted to be home under the damson tree with Ho-Ho.

When Henry finally woke up there was a beautiful lady dressed in blue holding his hand. Henry stared at her.

"Who are you?" he asked timidly, confused, with no idea where he might be.

The nurse smiled sweetly. "My name is Angel," she said.

"Am I in Heaven?" Henry asked, almost to himself, "And is my friend Ho-Ho here?" he added, becoming more cheerful.

"You are in hospital," explained Nurse Angel. "You have had a nasty fall and bumped your head. We are going to help you get better."

Henry was downcast again. "But I have to go home and find my friend Ho-Ho," he explained.

"Tell me all about your friend," said Angel in such a lovely soft voice that Henry could not resist. Normally Henry would not talk about Ho-Ho to a stranger, but this was somehow different and he could tell that Angel was a very special person. Henry told her everything, though perhaps not very clearly as his head hurt a lot and some bits of the story were a little confused.

"I just want to see Ho-Ho," he finally said, tears running down his cheeks.

When he finally looked up at Angel, she too had tears in her eyes.

"Some day, Henry, I would love to have a little boy like you. Your friend Ho-Ho is very lucky to have such a wonderful friend."

"No!" said Henry raising his voice. "No!" and he added very quietly, "I am so lucky to have had Ho-Ho as my friend," and sank into a deep sleep.

Through her tears, Nurse Angel wrote her notes for the doctor.

** **

"We are still very worried about him," said the doctor in the white coat to Henry's mother. "At first we thought he was recovering quite well from his very nasty fall, but he keeps talking about some elephant that lives up a tree. The nurse's report makes very interesting reading indeed. He seems upset and cries all the time he's awake. It's almost as though Henry doesn't want to get better."

"Is there anything I can do?" asked Henry's mother.

"Nothing at all, I'm afraid," sighed the doctor, "You did everything just perfectly. When you find someone unconscious, you must make sure they are breathing all right and then call an ambulance. I'm afraid it is out of your hands now. I just wish I could see into his little mind and understand why he is so upset."

** **

After a while Henry woke up. It must have been nearly midnight; and for once the hospital was fairly quiet, which was nice. His head still hurt a lot from the accident. That would teach him not to climb! Everything about his fall and the journey to hospital was jumbled and confused, and had there really been an Angel there when he had first woken up in those stiff white hospital sheets? But where was Ho-Ho? The very thought of Ho-Ho missing brought tears to Henry's eyes once more.

"Where could he be?" wondered Henry. If only he could know that his friend was all right. Henry could not sleep; he could not bear the thought of his friend being in some kind of trouble. Suddenly there was a tap, tapping at the window. Henry could not believe his ears! It was Ho-Ho's special tap! He dashed over to the window and sure enough, there was Ho-Ho, looking at him, smiling as though nothing had happened. "Ho-Ho," whispered Henry, hardly able to contain himself, "Are you all right?"

"Yes," replied Ho-Ho, "When are you coming back home?" Henry would have hugged his enormous friend, but the windows were always locked. "Where were you, Ho-Ho?" cried Henry, "I couldn't find you anywhere!"

"I couldn't sleep with all that noise of grass cutting," said Ho-Ho, a little upset by his friend's tone of voice, "So I moved into the pear tree next door. I must have overslept," he added sheepishly.

"I was so worried about you, Ho-Ho. I thought you might be in trouble and need help so I was climbing the tree and then everything went black and I think I bumped my head – so I'm here in hospital and ..."

Henry had to stop as the thought of his friend being injured brought tears to his eyes again.

"You risked hurting yourself to help me?" asked Ho-Ho in a puzzled voice. "But why, Henry? I'm only an elephant."

"You are the very best friend that a boy could have," said Henry simply. "Besides, there are lots of boys like me, but there is only one Ho-Ho."

As Henry promised to get well and meet his friend tomorrow, the darkness hid the large tears that welled up in Ho-Ho's eyes.

"Yes indeed! A most remarkable recovery," the doctor explained to Henry's mother. "A most remarkable recovery. We had planned to keep him in here for at least a week, but after seeing him this morning I'm sure he will be OK to go home today. However," he added looking very serious, "Do make sure he rests a lot and bring him straight back if you are worried."

"Oh yes!" said his mother, overjoyed at having Henry back. "I will do anything you say. It is just wonderful to be taking him home. Do you get many surprises like this?"

"Nothing surprises me any more," replied the doctor wearily, "For instance, last night I had just stitched someone's arm and was going back to bed shortly after midnight, when," he lowered his voice and moved a little closer, "I could have sworn I saw a huge elephant looking into one of the hospital windows!"

The two grown-ups laughed together. What a silly thought!

Introduction to Healing Stories

As a full-time family doctor for 35 years, it has been a continual source of amazement to me how the mind of the patient can greatly influence the outcome of an illness. One has only to look at the remarkable effects of dummy tablets (placebos) to be convinced that what the patient experiences emotionally, and what he or she believes, can powerfully alter the outcome of a disorder. Moreover, having employed clinical hypnosis for 30 years and hypnotised away warts and nasal polyps, and controlled bleeding and pain, I can attest from personal experience as to the power of suggestion!

The reading of the bedtime story is potentially an excellent setting in which to help your child by suggestion, and as my experience grew (very slowly!) of using bedtime stories to help children, I am now more convinced than ever that this very powerful tool can help your child in so many different ways.

The following stories were written to help children with particular problems and the context in which they were written is outlined in my notes which preface each story. If your child has one of the problems in these stories, just take a few minutes beforehand to alter the details of the child in the story to fit your own child. If you think that a new story might help your child's problem, just drop me a line and I will try to write a 'special' story to help!

Now retired from full-time practice, it is my dream to help as many children as possible with 'healing' bedtime stories. Thank you for being part of that dream.

Uncle Samson's Strange Gift

Author's note: In the middle of a busy surgery many years ago, Mrs L brought her 7-year-old daughter, Sarah, to see me. Since the death of her next-door neighbour, Sarah had been worried about people dying and didn't like her Mum being out of sight; they had great difficulty getting her to go out in the car. Sarah also had nightmares and panics. What could I do as a harassed G.P. to help Sarah? In desperation I gave her some of my Henry and Ho-Ho stories, asking mum to read Sarah one story each night and to report back on how Sarah liked them. Mum reported that Sarah loved the stories, so I wrote a special story for Sarah – Uncle Samson's Strange Gift – which cured her immediately! This was the start of my efforts to help children through the medium of bedtime stories. Although it was written to try to help Sarah cope with the death of her next-door neighbour, I hoped that it might help other children cope with death or separation.

The tap, tapping sound was not coming from the window. Besides, it was far too early to be Ho-Ho.

"Henry," said his mother, gently tapping on the bedroom door, "Are you awake yet?"

Henry stretched and peered at his mother through sleepy eyes.

"There is a letter for you, Henry, and it is marked 'very urgent'," she declared, handing him an important-looking envelope.

"Now do tell me if you don't understand it, and I'll explain it to you."

She waited for a moment, expecting Henry to open the envelope, but Henry slowly drifted back to sleep, wondering who could be writing to him very urgently. Perhaps Patrick the policeman was having trouble with a difficult case, or perhaps someone needed rescuing, or perhaps ...

When he awakened from the sleep, his mother had gone. Henry opened the letter. It certainly looked very important, but Henry was very saddened by the contents: his dear old friend Uncle Samson had died. The letter put things in a very complicated way, but that was the long and short of it. Tears welled up in his eyes as he remembered the amazing old man with his crackly old laugh and his fund of quite extraordinary stories. Uncle Samson had certainly had more adventures than any other person could possibly have had! Henry began to remember some of them and the way Uncle Samson told them, with those knowing winks and pauses that kept Henry spellbound.

He was awakened from his memories of Uncle Samson by voices downstairs. It was his friend Bridget! Henry quickly got out of bed and slipped into his clothes. Henry was very fond of Bridget, who was the same age as himself and always happy and smiling, and he was looking forward to seeing her.

"Is anything the matter?" asked his mother as he appeared in the kitchen, still clutching the letter, "Have you been crying, Henry?" she asked.

"Not really," said Henry, as his mother had so many things to worry about, he truly didn't want to bother her.

"Good," said his mother. "Now, Bridget has had some bad news this morning as her father has had to go away, so I've asked her round to play with you. Why don't you take your drinks out into the garden and decide what you are going to do together?"

"So I just don't know how long he will be away for and I need him to be here," Bridget finally declared, obviously very sad at the sudden absence of her father. Henry nodded sympathetically; Bridget was usually so happy and cheerful, that he couldn't bear to see her hurting like this.

"What's that in your hand?" she said, finally noticing the very important envelope that Henry was clutching. In sharing Bridget's sadness, Henry had completely forgotten his own. Rather than try to explain, he handed it to her. Her forehead wrinkled in concentration as she read through the whole of the letter. Finally she put it down on the grass, folded her arms, shook her head and smiled; she looked like the familiar confident Bridget again.

"You really are amazing, Henry!" she declared in quiet admiration. Apparently, the letter was not just to let Henry know about Uncle Samson's death, but also to tell him about his will. Before he died, Uncle Samson had written down what he wanted to be done with all his possessions – this is called a 'will' – and Henry and someone called Ho-Ho were to be given everything! The letter told them to visit solicitors in the city to collect what Uncle Samson had left for them.

"But how can we get to the place? And who is Ho-Ho?" Bridget asked, apparently defeated.

Henry made a quick decision. Normally he didn't tell people about his special magic friend, but this was, after all, quite an unusual circumstance.

"Ho-Ho is a magic elephant and the very best friend a boy could have," he finally declared. "Ho-Ho will take us to the solicitors."

Bridget became even more amazed, "Where does Ho-Ho live?" she asked.

"In this tree!" Henry said, pointing upwards.

Bridget began to laugh at the very idea of an elephant living in a tree.

"He does too!" said Henry going a little red and, peering up into the branches, he called out, "Come down, Ho-Ho, come down!"

The two friends peered up into the tree for what seemed like ages. Suddenly there was a 'plop' as a tiny elephant fell from the tree. Bridget watched in amazement as the tiny creature grew and grew into an enormous smiling elephant.

"Hello," said Ho-Ho sheepishly and looking so incredibly funny that Bridget began to laugh. Soon all three of them were quite helpless with laughter.

** **

The journey into the city was the most enjoyable trip of Bridget's entire life. Hanging on to Ho-Ho and seeing the streets from so high up would have been funny enough, but the looks of amazement and disbelief from everyone they passed were a joy to behold. They had to ask instructions several times before they found the right place, but finally they arrived. Henry had heard of 'solicitors' before, but he thought they were something to do with the police; he was most surprised to discover that they were also the people who actually took charge of people's wills after they had died.

The solicitor's office was a rather dingy place set above some shops. Bridget was worried that Ho-Ho would have to stay in the street, but of course when the coast was clear he simply shrank down to his small size and slipped into Henry's pocket.

The solicitor himself, Mr Davenport, was at first quite amazed when Henry introduced himself, expecting someone much older. "And you must be Ho-Ho," he said shaking hands with Bridget.

The two friends looked at each other and giggled.

"Well, it's like this," he said, cleaning his glasses and looking up at the ceiling, "Samson was not a very rich man. In fact, he was actually quite poor, and after everything has been sorted out, all that remains is, in fact, that!" He pointed a thumb at a large wooden trunk in the corner of the room. "I've had a look through the contents and frankly they are rubbish, pure rubbish! However," he added looking up with a smile, "Sam's brother Boris will pay you £100 for the thing, and frankly, if I were you, I would take it. You children could buy a lot with that."

"£100," thought Henry, trying to work out how much ice-cream £100 would buy. He was silent for a minute. "No thanks," he finally declared, "Just help us down the stairs with the trunk."

Henry smiled at Bridget as the look of disbelief on her face slowly changed to a smile of understanding.

Later, under the damson tree, the three friends were in high spirits recalling the day's adventures and going through the contents of the trunk. Certainly the contents would seem to be rubbish to anyone else, but each item reminded Henry of one of Uncle Samson's amazing stories.

There was the eye patch he had worn when he was bitten by the buzz-fly in the Amazon jungle and had nearly been eaten by cannibals; the feather from the shrike eagle of Umteng when he had fallen from the Camaz Ridge; and the invisibility powder, which he had stolen from a tribe of ferocious Indians in Central America. Somehow he had never had to use the invisibility powder as his enormous strength "always got me out of trouble," he had told Henry. Bridget was amazed at Uncle Samson's stories; the adventures sounded so incredible and his escapes were nothing short of miraculous.

"Yes! That's the word I couldn't remember," said Henry, "Miraculous. Uncle Samson always wore a belt with real diamonds in it which he said protected him at all times from danger. The miraculous belt of Archops he called it!" Henry looked pleased with himself, then added thoughtfully, "I wonder what happened to it."

He dipped his hand into the bottom of the trunk and pulled out, to everyone's total amazement, an old, well-worn black belt, which could only be Uncle Samson's miraculous belt!"

"If those diamonds are real," said Bridget, "They will be worth a fortune!"

The two friends looked at each other for a full minute and then slowly shook their heads together; they both knew that somewhere Uncle Samson could see them treasuring his old belongings, treasuring his stories, treasuring his memories. Even though his death was fresh in their minds, he would have been overjoyed to see the three friends being so happy on his account.

Henry looked at Ho-Ho and realised how happy his life was. "You make me very happy, Ho-Ho," he said.

"Me too," said Ho-Ho, "Even when we aren't together."

He looked so funny and serious that Bridget and Henry began to laugh, and Ho-Ho laughed too, until tears ran right down all their cheeks. In their laughter they understood how people who love you want to make you happy, even when they are far apart from you, and if you really love them you remember all the wonderful times and let them make you happy too.

That night Bridget's mother returned. Bridget was happier than she could ever remember. She seemed to have learnt so much today. She felt that she could never feel quite so lonely and frightened ever again. She had two new friends and knew that her mother and father loved her very much and wanted her to be happy, even if they were sometimes away from her.

"My word," said her mother, hugging Bridget, "You do seem to have grown up today!"

And Bridget knew that she really had.

A Very, Very Hot Day

Author's Note: This story was written to try to help a very intelligent 5-year-old girl called Molly who had very bad eczema. She was under specialist care and was using strong creams and ointments for her skin. Molly thoroughly enjoyed the stories and her skin improved significantly, though it was impossible to say whether it was the stories that made the difference. The stories definitely altered Molly's attitude to her skin problem, and she become far less agitated and upset about it (prior to the stories she used to cry a lot and ask why God had given her this problem). Henry and Ho-Ho also helped when she woke up at night and the feelings from the magic well made her feel better too.

Henry and Ho-Ho were sitting under the damson tree, drinking their orange juice. It was a happy morning, very sunny, with a beautiful day stretching out before them.

"I wonder what will happen today?" said Henry looking up at the sky. "One thing is for sure; it is definitely not going to rain!" Ho-Ho nodded; the most certain thing of all was that it would definitely not rain.

"Another thing for certain is that I won't have any play friends today!" added Henry. Although Henry was very happy with his friend Ho-Ho, he sometimes missed having friends of his own age nearby. Ho-Ho did understand the problem. They sat a while in silence.

"Henry! Henry!" The voice of Henry's mother came ringing from the house. "Quick," whispered Henry, "Back up into your tree, Ho-Ho". In a flash the huge elephant had disappeared, and Henry's mother came from the house with a small girl.

"This," she announced, "is Molly. She is a ..., well actually, a sort of cousin of yours, Henry. I want you two to have a nice day together and I want you to be on your very best behaviour, Henry. Molly has come here to help her skin get better and she needs some nice, quiet company." She glared at Henry for a moment to be sure that he understood his task. Then she smiled at both the children, "... And here is your picnic basket for the day. I don't expect to hear another sound from you until you come in for supper!"

The two children looked at each other in silence. Henry had heard about Molly. In general, Henry was very well-mannered, but he did slip up occasionally and, when he did, his mother always said something like, "Now Molly wouldn't speak to her mother in that way. Molly is a very well-mannered child!"

As you may imagine, Henry was not keen to meet this wonderful girl who sounded no fun at all, and certainly not the kind of person who would come on adventures with him and Ho-Ho.

Molly, too, had heard some rather strange tales about Henry – that he spent hours under the damson tree on his own talking to himself, that he had some very odd friends, that he would disappear for hours on end and that he had some very strange adventures for a small boy.

As Henry looked at Molly, he noticed some redness on her skin. "What is that redness on your skin?" asked Henry. "Does it hurt?"

"It's called eczema," said Molly. "It is because of allergies and that is why I have to have a special diet with no milk and stuff."

Henry was becoming curious now.

"Yes," continued Molly, "And I have to put lots of funny creams on it. It's very nice of you to ask."

Henry was becoming even more curious.

"I get it in lots of places," said Molly, showing Henry the backs of her knees and the front of her elbows, where the eczema looked especially bad.

"Do you cry a lot with it?" Henry asked.

"No!" said Molly with a smile, "It burns sometimes, but I am very brave!"

Henry stared with admiration at Molly and these unexpected revelations. It would have been wonderful to have an adventure with this brave girl, but ...

"What shall we do today?" asked Molly.

Henry looked sadly at the floor. "I suppose we will just sit here and have a picnic," he said reluctantly.

"Oh!" sighed Molly, "I was so hoping that we'd do something exciting. I've heard a lot about you."

The two cousins stared at each other and slowly began to smile, and then began to laugh together for no very good reason at all.

"Can you keep a very special secret?" Henry finally asked, looking questioningly at Molly, but he already knew in his heart that here was someone he could trust with his big secret.

When he had explained about Ho-Ho and a few of their adventures, Molly began to understand the odd things she had heard about Henry, but the truth was far more interesting than anything she could ever have imagined.

"You can come down now, Ho-Ho," Henry whispered up into the tree.

Soon there was a tiny 'plop', and later still a huge smiling elephant was sitting on the grass.

Although the three friends were getting along famously, there was obviously something bothering Ho-Ho.

"What is that redness on your skin?" he finally blurted out. Molly explained patiently that it was something called 'eczema' and that she needed a special diet and creams for it.

"Yes, and she is very brave indeed!" said Henry.

"I think I have got 'eggsymar'," said Ho-Ho, "But I've never seen it. I think I have some on my back!" he added, indicating with his trunk the exact spot.

"Yes, look at this, Molly" said Henry, "Ho-Ho has a patch just like yours and he's never seen it!"

Henry had an idea; he told his friends to wait and he disappeared into the house, returning a few minutes later with some old mirrors he'd retrieved from Uncle Samson's chest. By positioning the mirrors in the right way, he could show Ho-Ho his patch of eczema. Ho-Ho was delighted, not so much at seeing his back for the first time, but seeing his own face in the mirror for the very first time also. He thought it was hilarious and for a while the three friends were helpless with laughter.

"Yes," thought Henry, "Molly is a wonderful companion for an adventure. We'll see where Uncle Dennis' balloon wants to take us!"

Soon they were floating high above the clouds in a most wonderful happy mood. Ho-Ho kept on looking in the mirror, making strange faces and laughing, and Molly hadn't felt so excited for ages. It was such a beautiful day and the sun became hotter and hotter. They opened the picnic basket and fortunately there were three large bottles of juice – one for each of the friends. How wonderful to be drifting and dreaming above the clouds, happy, excited and curious.

Henry learned a lot more about his new friend and was told he should call her "Moll" for short now that they knew each other. She had a goldfish called Mr Greedie and she could sing and dance. She could even do a dance called a 'tap dance', which impressed Henry enormously as he would surely fall off if he tried to dance on a tap!

Finally the balloon began to descend and as they came down beneath the clouds they could see the land below – it was pure sand – a boiling hot desert. As they reached closer to the ground the heat became very strong and soon the balloon was nestling into the soft sand.

"What do we do now?" asked Molly.

Henry thought for a minute. "We can't stay here or we'll frizzle!" he said. "We must find some shade and some more drinks!"

"You can leave me here," said Ho-Ho, "I'm still enjoying this mirror. I'll find you later."

So the two friends set off across the burning sand, each carrying just a bottle of juice.

After an hour or so, they were both feeling very uncomfortable and Henry was becoming rather grumpy. He stopped and looked all around.

"I think we should go that way," he said with a big gesture. Unfortunately he gestured with the arm that was carrying the juice, and it flew out of his hand and emptied itself on the desert sand.

"Oh dear!" wailed Henry, "I've nothing to drink now, and I'm so very thirsty!"

"Don't worry," replied Molly, calm and reassuring, "We can share mine!"

Henry was most impressed with his friend's calmness and kindness in this serious situation.

After what seemed like hours, the friends finally spied something rather different on the horizon. It looked like an outcrop of rock, which would certainly give them some shelter from the sun. They quickly made haste towards it. As they approached it two children, a girl and a boy, came out to meet them.

"You must be thirsty," said the girl, "Have some of this!" She handed a flask to Henry who guzzled down some of the drink without saying a word. It was the most beautiful drink he had ever had in his life, made from strange desert fruits, as he later discovered. Molly also took a long swig.

"Thank you!" said Henry.

"You saved our lives," added Molly.

They followed the two children into the oasis, which stretched like a huge green field behind the rocky outcrop. Soon there were more children, all keen to talk and ask questions.

"How did you get here?" asked the girl. Henry had learned to be very cautious about telling strangers the complete truth.

"We just walked!" he said. All the children began to laugh, though Henry could not understand why. "You are not telling the truth!" cried the girl. All the other children seemed to agree with her.

Molly and Henry quickly discovered the first big secret of the oasis: that it was quite impossible to tell lies in that place! They knew that fear makes one's face go white, and embarrassment makes you blush, but here in this place, all the changes were greatly magnified, so what they were feeling could be instantly recognised by all the children. No choice at all then but to tell the children the whole truth.

The children were amazed to hear Henry's story. It was a beautiful, wondrous place and drinking the fruit juice made the children feel wonderful. Suddenly the calmness was interrupted by a loud shriek: "They're back, they're back!" came a terrified voice. The children all ran off shouting and banging things. The girl turned and looked back at Henry and Molly.

"All our parents are away at the Majesty Meeting, and we have to protect the oasis against the rathoppers!" she said, running towards the noise.

Henry and Molly followed the shouting children until they saw them – huge rat-like creatures leaping over the walls, eating everything in sight. The noise from the children did not seem to be helping and the rathoppers were taking over this oasis paradise. The poor children! Their homes were in real trouble.

Suddenly there was a deafening sound from the skies. Everyone looked up, terrified, to see a balloon above the oasis, with an elephant's trunk sticking out of it making a deafening trumpeting sound. There were flashing lights coming from the balloon too, as Ho-Ho had been playing with the mirror and had learned how to reflect the sunlight.

**  **

The rathoppers were even more terrified than the children and in a trice had sped off back into the desert.

As the balloon descended, the children all gathered round and applauded as the very hot elephant climbed out.

"How did you know to make the trumpeting sound?" asked Henry.

Ho-Ho looked rather hurt. "I was singing," he said, "I always sing when I am lonely or worried. I am also very thirsty," he added.

There were peals of laughter as the children took turns in giving drinks to the very thirsty elephant! In return, Ho-Ho showed everyone all the tricks he had learned with the mirrors, showing them how they could reflect the sunshine and produce dazzling lights and bright spots on faraway objects.

The friends soon fell into a deep and exhausted sleep, a wonderful refreshing sleep that seemed to last for hours. Henry was finally awakened by the girl giving him a nudge. "We think the rathoppers will be coming back soon," she said rather nervously. "Can you get your elephant ready to make his noise to scare them off?"

Henry nodded and looked at Molly. They would soon have to leave and take Ho-Ho with them; how would the children manage on their own against the rathoppers then? They sank into deep thought.

"It might help," said Molly, "If we let the children have Ho-Ho's mirrors; at least then they will be able to make the flashes when the rathoppers come again!"

They told the girl of their plan and the mirrors were set up ready. But how could they make those loud noises if Ho-Ho wasn't with them?

Then Molly noticed that the children were all wearing wooden shoes, which the children called 'clogs'. "Could I try a pair of your wooden shoes on?" she asked. Then she noticed that all the huts had iron rooftops to keep off the sun and rain. Molly suddenly had an idea.

"Gather round, all you children!" she cried as she climbed onto one of the rooftops. Then she began to tap-dance. The children were intrigued with the rhythm and the noise of the wooden shoes on the iron roof. Soon they were all trying it and they quickly learned this new dance. The noise was deafening!

Finally they all collapsed, exhausted and thirsty, and had a long drink of the beautiful oasis fruit drink, before falling into a deep sleep once again.

** **

"Look out, everybody, the rathoppers are coming back! Quick, everyone!" Somebody yelled, waking the three friends from their peaceful sleep.

Molly jumped into action. "On the rooftops, everyone," she yelled, climbing onto the roof and starting her tap dance. Ho-Ho began to flash his mirror and the children began to dance. The noise of the clogs on the tin roofs was like thunder and even louder than the trumpeting of a thirsty elephant. The rathoppers were terrified, the leaders turning and running into the ones behind them. Each rathopper turned and ran in terror back into the desert. In no time at all peace was restored.

"You can keep our mirrors," said Henry, "You need them more than we do!"

One of the girls came over to Molly. "Your idea of the roof dance and the mirrors saved us all; you are a heroine. Come with me!"

She took her deep into the middle of the oasis, where there was a tiny spring. The light filtered strangely through the trees.

"This place is called 'All-is-Well' and the children come here when they are ill. Here the light is very special and helps to cure the skin. You have hot skin, like all the desert children and after being here and feeling the calm, your skin will heal better." Molly felt quite strange. The light, the girl's voice, the excitement of the day and the feelings of her skin healing and getting better all made her feel very calm and relaxed. After a while she knew that these feelings would carry on even after she arrived home.

In the balloon on the way home, with the sun going down and the feeling of peace and calmness, Molly felt so good and proud of herself. Her skin stayed cool and comfortable. She knew she had learned some amazing secrets that would always be hers. For ever and ever and ever!

Good People Help Each Other!

Author's Note: There is a massive problem of childhood obesity in our society and its consequences will inevitably be serious and far-reaching. I feel very sorry for these children whose lack of self-esteem and poorer quality of life is quite apparent; but what can be done? This story is an attempt to help such children. If you wish to use it, I'd suggest that you get everything else set up first – a healthy food regime, healthy snacks and some kind of suitable exercise programme. I'd suggest also that the child in the story is not identical with your child, but that it would be easy for your child to identify with the character in the story (i.e. be subtle and don't make it too 'full on'!). Please feel free to contact me at any stage if you are using this story; the subject is such a huge and painful one that any learning we can share will be invaluable!

Henry was friendly with many children, but most them lived quite far away. In fact, this was a very happy arrangement, because he never knew which of his friends might suddenly arrive and how long they might stay.

One such friend was Bertie. At first, they had not got on very well at all, as Bertie kept on talking about 'video games', which Henry knew nothing about. How well Henry remembered the expression on Bertie's face when he had asked, "What are video games?" Bertie had looked totally astonished, and had looked so funny that Henry and Ho-Ho had been helpless with laughter.

But Bertie really wanted to be friends with Henry and Ho-Ho, and quickly dropped the subject of video games. Instead he talked about history and ancient peoples, battles, wars and the various tragedies that had befallen them. He also had a wonderful ability to describe how people had lived in ancient times and how they had managed to survive. Bertie also knew about the earth: about volcanoes, earthquakes and tornadoes. In fact, there was very little that Bertie didn't know about, and he could make anything sound interesting anyway!

"You must be the most popular boy in your class!" said Henry one day after listening to one of Bertie's amazing stories. There was a silence for a while, and Henry was sure that a little tear appeared in Bertie's eye.

"You looked sad when I said that," said Henry, "You do have lots and lots of friends, don't you?" he asked.

Bertie thought for a while. "They call me 'fatty', or sometimes 'porky'. The children at school are not as nice as you, Henry. They tease me because I am … well, fat!"

Oddly enough, Henry had hardly noticed that Bertie was fat, because he was such good company and always seemed to be happy. Now he noticed and realised how awful it must be to be teased by your school friends.

"Would you like to be thinner?" asked Henry.

"Yes," said Bertie thoughtfully, "But I really don't know how. I am hungry a lot of the time, but I don't seem to eat a lot more than the other children. Maybe you and Ho-Ho can help?"

Henry felt very proud. This wonderful boy who seemed to know so much about so many things had a problem that he and Ho-Ho might fix! But how?

"What do you think, Ho-Ho?" asked Henry.

Ho-Ho thought for a little while. "Elephants don't really get fat," said Ho-Ho. "Even birds don't get fat," he added thoughtfully, "And they eat more than any other creature!"

This seemed rather puzzling to the boys, but Ho-Ho explained that birds really did eat more than all the other animals, but because they only ate 'natural' foods such as fruit, nuts and insects, and, because they had to fly around all day burning off energy, they never got fat!

"Well, I'm certainly not going to start eating insects!" said Bertie, and as Henry and Ho-Ho burst into peals of laughter, he added, "And I certainly don't think I will be able to learn to fly!" And all three friends laughed together.

"But some animals are very fat," said Henry, "Such as pigs!"

Bertie looked very thoughtful. "In fact wild pigs, which are called 'boars', are very thin," Bertie told him. "They are also quite fierce and can run very quickly. It is only the pigs on the farm which are fat; these are fed on special fattening foods and don't have to run around in the forest looking for things to eat!"

"Well, that's it!" said Henry, "We just have to find out about natural foods!"

Ho-Ho looked rather sheepish. "Does that mean I'll have to stop eating ice-cream?"

If you have ever seen an elephant looking sheepish, you will understand why Henry and Bertie were helpless with laughter.

So the plan was agreed: they were to go to the market and find out about natural foods. The two boys helped Ho-Ho with his roller skates, clambered onto his back and made themselves comfortable for the long journey. Henry had remembered a wonderful outdoor market in a small village that would be perfect to find out about these natural foods.

The market was buzzing with sounds: noises of music, laughter and people shouting about what they were trying to sell. There was even a roundabout for the children. Henry and Bertie made several enquiries as to where

they might be able to find some 'natural foods' and eventually found themselves at a very quiet stall, which they seemed to have all to themselves! The owner of the stall was an old lady called Ruth, and her 'assistant' was her grand-daughter called Kate. The three friends were soon talking to Ruth and Kate, and developed an instant liking for them. Kate was a little older than Henry and Bertie, but was full of energy and enthusiasm, and so keen to talk with the three friends. Ruth seemed to know everything about natural foods; about where they came from and how good they were for your health. It was such a shame that there didn't seem to be many people buying from their stall.

"Why aren't you busier here?" asked Henry.

"I've no idea," said Ruth, "The foods that I sell are so good for your health and energy, you would think that people would be queuing up to buy them!"

The three friends were very enthusiastic about all their discoveries about these natural foods, and would dearly have loved to help Ruth and Kate with their business. They would have bought a lot of natural foods for themselves, but they had no money with them. Instead they decided to explore the market, and what fun it all was! Lots of people seemed to know Henry from previous adventures there, but everyone was so friendly and nice. It made the friends very sad that people weren't more interested in these natural foods.

"I'm starving hungry," said Bertie, "Can you smell all those wonderful food smells?" Henry and Ho-Ho could certainly smell lots of wonderful smells that made them feel hungry too, but they had no money to buy anything.

"That's it," said Bertie finally, "If only Ruth and Kate had some nice smells of food coming from their stall, people would queue up to buy from them!"

At last the three friends had an idea that might help their new friends! They rushed back to the stall to share their ideas with Ruth and Kate. At first they were greeted with silence. Then Ruth pointed out that healthy foods don't usually smell very nice – they usually smell of nothing!

Kate looked thoughtful. "Granny, you used to make a beautiful soup that smelt wonderful, and I'm sure you said that it was full of goodness and healthy ingredients!"

Slowly the plan emerged: they would bring a giant pan from their home, and make the soup right there and then! Ruth knew the names of the healthy ingredients that would make it smell nice, and the beautiful aroma might well attract some people to buy from their stall. The problem was that Ruth could not leave the stall, and there were lots of ingredients that needed to be brought from their home, which was over a mile away. Fortunately there were two bikes available and it was agreed that Kate and Bertie would ride to their home and bring the pan and all the ingredients back with them. Henry was not allowed to ride a bike because of a previous misadventure with a squirrel and an old pair of pyjamas, so it was left to Bertie and Ruth.

** **

Bringing all the ingredients from home took several journeys, and at the end of it Bertie was hot and exhausted. But even before the final ingredients were put into the pan, there were several people around the stall, attracted by the smell.

Ruth had an audience now and was in full cry, explaining about the value of natural foods and how the soup she had made was full of natural goodness. And of course, people attract crowds, and the numbers grew and grew. When the soup was finally cooked, so many people wanted to try it! Ruth ladled out a cup of soup for the people at the front and as they tasted it, she explained about all the wonderful ingredients that had gone into its making. They drank it slowly, savouring every mouthful and although they wanted more, there was not enough for second helpings – everyone wanted to try the fabulous soup. Not only that, but while they were waiting for their taste of the soup, they spent money on the other things for sale at the stall. The sales that day were the best they had ever had!

The afternoon passed quickly, and Ruth and Kate were delighted at the amount of money that they had taken.

"Could I please try some soup?" asked Bertie very politely, controlling the fact that he was extremely hungry. Ruth was shocked.

"My poor child," she said giving him a hug, "You have saved our business; you can have anything you want!"

The soup that Bertie enjoyed that day was the most wonderful food he had ever tasted in his entire life. He drank it slowly and was aware of what wonderful power this natural food had for him. Perhaps it was because he was really very hungry as well, and that he had done a lot of hard work on the bike helping to rescue the business. Ruth gave him lots of advice afterwards about how to drink healthy drinks with meals and about the power you get from fruit and vegetables.

She also gave him lots of free natural foods – and Henry and Ho-Ho too of course.

On the way back home on Ho-Ho's back, Bertie felt absolutely wonderful. He had discovered natural foods, which he realised were power foods that would make him stronger, fitter and slimmer. Kate had been so grateful, she had kissed him on the cheek and made him feel even more special. Today he had been a hero for the first time, but he was to be a hero many more times in the future. Over the next few years, Bertie would become one of the most popular children the school had ever known, and would do well at sports and in his tests, but he knew it all began with the amazing adventure with Henry and Ho-Ho.

Henry, Ho-Ho and the Bug Flies

Author's Note: Warts in children are pretty common and are a nuisance to remove. Yet they do disappear by using suggestion – everyone has heard of "charming warts away" and the various 'old wives' tales that have reputedly worked; I myself have hypnotised warts away on several occasions! This story was written for a little girl who was distressed by her warts and didn't want to have them burned off. Unfortunately, the warts started to disappear while she was having the earlier Ho-Ho stories read and before she got to this 'wart-curing' story! If your child has warts, why not try this story, altering the details of Samantha to fit your own child. It is probably the best, and certainly the kindest, alternative treatment!

"But please don't call me Sam!" pleaded Henry's little cousin, "My name is Samantha!" Henry was very impressed by her definite opinions on what she should be called. "And please call me Henry," he responded in agreement. They were going to be good friends.

Samantha lived a long way away from Henry, so he rarely saw her, but as it happened, her parents were staying in the local town 'on business' and so it was arranged for Samantha to stay with Henry so that she would have someone to play with.

This was her first morning and already they were sitting under the damson tree having a late breakfast of rolls and honey and orange juice. She was talking about her school and her friends at her home in Ridgeley, and what she wanted to do when she grew up.

"And how do you spend your time?" she finally asked. Henry really didn't know what to say; he felt rather silly with this clever little girl who seemed to do so much.

"I sort of help to solve people's problems!" he finally said.

"What sort of problems?" asked Samantha, looking rather doubtful.

"All sorts ... all sorts of problems," said Henry, hoping she would change the subject.

"Yes, but what sorts of problems?" persisted Samantha. Henry scratched his head. "What sort have you got?" he finally asked.

Samantha laughed a lovely tinkling laugh. "I don't have any problems at all," she said shaking her head. Then she stopped and looked serious, "Apart from these. Look!"

She held her hand out to Henry; it had some strange shiny lumps on it.

"What are they?" asked Henry, never having seen anything like them at all before.

"They are called 'warts'," said Samantha with an air of wisdom, "And nothing can make them go away, apart from having them burned off, and I certainly don't want that! I have been to the doctor and he has tried with creams, but nothing can make them go, and I hate them – they look horrible."

Samantha knew lots of information about warts and Henry listened with great interest. It seems that they are caused because tiny little creatures called viruses sometimes get into the skin and grow into a big spot. Although they don't damage the person in any way, they look horrible. Finally they just go away, but in the meantime, nothing works very well (apart from burning them away) and you just have to put up with them.

"Shall I get my magnifying glass, so that we can see these tiny creatures?" asked Henry. Samantha burst out laughing, "You can't see them with a magnifying glass," she giggled, "Viruses are very, very tiny bugs indeed!"

Henry very much wanted to show Samantha that he was interesting and clever, but he had no idea how to tackle things too small even to see!

"Can girls keep secrets?" he asked, looking at her very carefully.

"Some girls can't keep secrets, but I can. In fact there are some secrets I can't even tell you, Henry."

"All right," whispered Henry, "Here comes my big secret!"

Henry began to tap gently on the tree and called quietly for his friend Ho-Ho. "It's okay to come down," he whispered up into the branches. Samantha looked on, amazed by this strange behaviour. Suddenly there was a 'plop' and a small object fell from the tree and landed on the grass. Soon it began to grow bigger and bigger until it was a fully-grown, smiling elephant. Ho-Ho looked very sleepy and was rubbing his eyes with his huge limbs. He looked so funny that Henry began to laugh, and that made Ho-Ho start laughing and, finally overcoming her astonishment, Samantha began to laugh too. Soon all three of them were crying with laughter.

"This is Samantha," Henry finally managed to announce, "She is my cousin and has invisible bugs that are all on her skin and make it lumpy," he said, to make her sound more interesting.

"They are called warts," added Samantha, "And nothing can make them better!"

"I bet Ho-Ho can!" said Henry, "Can't you, Ho-Ho?"

The poor elephant looked so puzzled and sleepy that the two children burst into laughter once again.

"I need to wake up first," said Ho-Ho, "Let's go for a ride in the balloon!"

"Would you like that?" Henry asked Samantha.

"I'd really love to go riding in the sky," she said, with great enthusiasm.

Ho-Ho smiled a mischievous happy smile. "That's settled then!" he said.

Soon the three friends were high above the clouds, bobbing along in Uncle Dennis' huge balloon.

"This is wonderful," cried Samantha, her eyes wide open with delight. "This is far, far better than any of my secrets!"

The balloon, as always, seemed to have a mind of its own, and after what seemed like hours, it began to slowly descend from the sky. Soon Henry could see a beautiful island nestling in the blue sea. It looked familiar and it seemed that they were heading for a very special island.

Even before the balloon landed, Samantha was amazed to see a crowd of children gathering in excitement and pointing up at them.

"It's Henry and Ho-Ho – they've come back!" one of the children cried.

Soon they had landed and the crowd of children were welcoming them with drinks. It was very warm and the three friends were very grateful for the drinks, which they drank very quickly indeed. Life always seemed so happy on the island and the children were obviously delighted to welcome Henry and Ho-Ho back. Samantha was soon established as a very welcome guest also – she had never felt so popular.

** **

Later, as they gathered around the campfire, Henry told of their latest adventures to a captive audience. The food, as usual, was wonderful and the happiness of the children was infectious.

"I like it here," said Ho-Ho contentedly. "But why," he puzzled, scratching his ear, "Has the balloon brought us here this time?"

Henry and Ho-Ho looked at each other wonderingly; they would soon find out.

As they sat and ate and talked, there was something bothering Henry, but he didn't know quite what it was.

"Is something different from the last time we were here?" he asked. The children all looked at each other before Lydia, the oldest of the group, spoke up.

"It might be the bug-flies?" she said.

That was it! The flies! They were small, brown insects and very irritating to the skin – and there were lots of them. In the excitement of arriving, Henry had not noticed them, but now he was very aware of them and how much they irritated the children, who were scratching wherever the flies landed. Perhaps that was why the balloon had landed on the island: it was up to Henry and Ho-Ho to rid the island of the bug-flies!

"How long have they been here?" asked Henry.

"Just a few weeks," explained Lydia, "But they seem to be increasing in numbers and we just don't know what to do to get rid of them."

"The only other slight problem," Lydia continued, "Is that we can't drink our cool water any more as it is full of small creatures."

The island, you see, had a spring in an underground cave that was sheltered from the sun, so it provided cool water at any time of the day, no matter how hot it was outside. There were many warm springs on the island, but no water tasted as good as the cool cave water.

Dusk was beginning to fall and suddenly all the flies were gone! It was so nice to be free from the itchy, ugly pests!

"Where have all the flies gone?" asked Henry.

"They just disappear at night," Lydia said simply, "Pity really, as they are luminous in the dark and easier to kill!" she added, laughing.

Henry and his friends fell into a wonderful deep sleep, even though his mind was still trying to grapple with the problem of the bug-flies.

An hour later Henry was wide-awake, thinking about the wonderful children and the bug-flies. He looked over at Ho-Ho and Samantha; they were also wide-awake and seemed to be thinking about the same problem.

"How can we get rid of the bug-flies?" Henry asked out loud.

Ho-Ho, remembering how helpless he felt when he was sleepy, said, "We must catch them when they are sleepy." The three friends thought for a while.

"That's it!" said Henry at last, "We must find out where they go at night and catch them there! But how can we find them in the dark?" he added helplessly.

"They are luminous," said Samantha, "That means that they glow in the dark and we should easily be able to find them!"

After a short discussion, the three friends decided to explore the island and find out where the bug-flies went at night. It was a brave decision, as the island had no lights, and away from the fire, it was pitch black apart from the light of the moon when it peeped from behind the clouds.

Everywhere on the island seemed to lead upwards to a central extinct volcano. The friends had taken off their shoes to make less noise, as they slowly made their way upwards. At first, the ground was sandy, but later they could feel a coarse grass under their feet. Occasionally they walked across small streams, which felt warm on their bare feet.

"What's that?" said Henry, startled by a strange animal noise in the distance.

"That's my friend the bird owl," said Ho-Ho smiling at a distant memory. Henry stopped, "Why do you call it a bird owl, Ho-Ho?" he asked.

"Because," said Ho-Ho thoughtfully, "That is its name. Everything has a name for a reason."

The friends continued. The flickering shadows as the moon appeared from behind the clouds cast an eerie light on the strange landscape. It made them feel as if they were being watched by a thousand eyes, peering out from each bush and tree. An occasional strange animal cry pierced the air and made the hair on the back of Samantha's neck stand on end.

After what seemed like hours, the friends were close to the top of the mountain and were obviously no further in their quest.

"We're getting nowhere," said Henry, "Let's have a rest and a think."

They sat down in silence, soothing their feet in a warm stream, each of the friends saddened by their lack of success. A cloud passed in front of the moon, and everything was totally still and silent.

"What's that noise?" asked Samantha. The friends listened attentively. Ho-Ho's ears were not only enormous, but also very, very sensitive.

"It's coming from down there," he finally said, "Follow me!" They followed him down through some thick bushes to a small clearing.

"Careful!" said Ho-Ho. There was a huge crack in the earth, quite big enough for a small child to fall into, and this was where the noise was coming from. The three friends peered down into its depths. There were the bug-flies, luminous, buzzing and diving in and out of the cold water at the bottom. The friends watched in total fascination, amazed by the extraordinary sight.

Back at the camp, Henry stared into the dying embers of the fire, totally baffled by the mysteries of the bug-flies.

"Have you ever seen anything like this before, Ho-Ho?" he asked.

"Hmmmm," said Ho-Ho, thoughtfully, "The flies remind me of hippos."

Henry and Samantha began to laugh. They had both seen the hippopotamus at the zoo; it was so huge that any connection with the bug-fly seemed quite silly.

"You see," went on Ho-Ho undeterred, "The hippo gets so hot, that he has to spend the whole time cooling down by sinking himself in rivers and mud!"

The friends thought for a while.

"Ho-Ho, you are a genius!" said Henry excitedly, "The flies become too hot and that's why they glow in the dark. That's why they need cool water at night to cool themselves down! If we could stop them getting to the cool water, they would have to go somewhere else!"

But how were they to do it? It would be impossible to seal off all the cracks in the earth to stop the flies getting in, and nobody knew where the cool water came from. It seemed impossible.

Samantha looked at her hand and stared sadly at the warts; both the problem of the flies and the problem of her warts seemed hopeless.

"What if we could warm up the cool water?" she finally said. "The bug-flies don't seem to like the warm water and they would probably leave the island and go somewhere else."

Then she remembered those streams of warm water, and a brilliant idea crossed her mind. She jumped up excitedly, "If we can channel one of those warm streams into that enormous crack where we nearly fell in, we can maybe warm up the cool water that way! Do you remember those warm streams?"

The friends did remember. They remembered the warm soothing water on their feet and how close it was to the bug-flies. This was the answer: it was time for action!

Henry woke all the children and told them to bring their spades, trowels and shovels – anything they could lay their hands on – to dig a trench. They trusted Henry so much, that the children didn't even question what he was doing. Soon they were high up on the mountain, digging away and making a channel to take the warm water into the huge crack. Ho-Ho, in spite of his huge size, was not very good at digging, but made himself useful by ensuring that none of the children fell into the crack in the darkness. Soon the job was done, and the warm water was gushing down into the darkness of the crack onto the bug-flies, making a beautiful sound.

"To the top of the mountain!" cried Henry and everyone followed him to the very summit. As Ho-Ho and all the children watched in the darkness there was not a sound to be heard, they just watched and waited. Soon there was a loud buzzing, humming noise and an enormous cloud of luminous flies emerged from the crack, hovering above for a few seconds and then speeding out across the sea. The children began to cheer, a cheer that lasted until the first flickerings of sunrise crept over the horizon.

Back in the balloon, soaring above the clouds, Samantha could scarcely believe what had happened. She was completely exhausted, but could scarcely sleep, remembering the excitement of her adventures. She knew she had been really helpful: it had been her idea to warm up the cool water. Perhaps Ho-Ho and Henry could solve any problem ... even her warts. After all they were only little bugs in the skin and, although she didn't want to have them burned off, she wouldn't mind them being warmed off. She asked Ho-Ho what he thought. Ho-Ho's voice was dreamy and made Samantha doze off. "Your skin warms up when you're excited or embarrassed," he droned on, as the gentle winds whispered around the balloon, "So if you let your skin warm up, your warts will get warmer and warmer. And as they get warmer and warmer, every day the warts gets smaller and smaller and smaller." It was just like a dream, but the warts did feel warmer and she felt absolutely sure that they were starting to go. Ho-Ho's voice droned on and Samantha felt just wonderful.

** **

Later that evening, Samantha and Henry were sitting having supper. Her mother and father had joined them for the meal.

"And what has my little girl being doing today?" Samantha's mother asked.

"Oh, nothing very much," replied Samantha, "We just sat and talked under the damson tree." She gave a knowing wink at Henry; he knew that his secret was safe with her.

As for Samantha, she felt happier than at any time in her life and, as she watched the warts disappear over the next few weeks, she grew in confidence and every day remembered her amazing adventure with Henry and Ho-Ho.

Joseph's Frightening Experience

Author's note: This story was used to help 7-year-old Joseph, who had been involved in a road traffic accident some 6 months previously. Following this he had nightmares, disturbed sleep and bedwetting, wouldn't sleep without the light on and also had panic attacks in certain traffic situations. Following use of the stories, especially the one below, his sleeping returned to normal and he slept right through the night; not only did all his other symptoms disappear, but he developed an interest in stories in general and the standard of his reading improved significantly.

In this case the character of Joseph in the story was identical with the real person, and if you wish to use this story to help your child recover from a bad experience, I'd suggest that you alter all the "Joseph" details to fit your own child. Good Luck!

Although they were not a very wealthy family, Henry's house was certainly large and his mother was very kind. She did quite a lot for local charities and, when people were in trouble, it was often to Henry's mother that they turned. So it happened that Mr and Mrs Rankin and their son Joseph came to stay at Henry's house 'for just a few weeks'.

Henry didn't mind too much, as Joseph was a little older than him and knew lots of interesting things. He was especially interesting when he talked about dinosaurs, but he was also a very good singer and impersonator. He also loved to be outside with Henry in the garden, so life was a lot better when Joseph was around.

However, today something was obviously quite wrong as Joseph did not seem like his old self at all; sometimes he would look into the distance and seem very sad, and he was far more nervous than usual.

Henry explained all this to Ho-Ho one morning while everyone was out shopping. "What can we do to help, Ho-Ho?" Henry asked.

Ho-Ho thought for a while; he had seen things like this before. Sometimes when a frightening thing happened to a person, it could leave them feeling very unhappy, even though the thing that caused it was well and truly over. Sometimes people didn't sleep so well as before and sometimes they didn't like to go to bed on their own. Henry was sure that Ho-Ho was right about Joseph. "But how can we help?" he asked his wise old friend.

"Bring him along to meet me," said Ho-Ho, "And perhaps an adventure will turn up; a good adventure can certainly take your mind off things."

"Yes indeed!" said Henry, nodding enthusiastically. The two friends certainly knew all about that!

** **

"You sure you can keep a secret?" said Henry to Joseph as they sat together under the damson tree.

"Yes, of course. I do sincerely promise," said Joseph, obviously not expecting anything special to keep a secret about.

"Ok, Ho-Ho, you can come down!" called out Henry.

In no time at all there sat a huge, smiling elephant, the biggest, happiest-looking elephant that Joseph had ever seen. Henry introduced them, and Ho-Ho watched Joseph with great attention.

"Now we are friends – proper friends – you can call me Joe," said Joseph.

"Well," said Henry, electing himself as the leader, "What are we going to do today?" The three friends sat in silence, each with their own thoughts. Suddenly something dropped from high up in the damson tree onto the ground. Henry explained about the magic balloon and soon they were gathered around the small lid and balloon with their eyes shut. Joe was surprised, in spite of Henry's warnings about what was happening. First the sound of rushing air, like air escaping from a tyre, then the feeling of dizziness and floating.

"We'll open our eyes after I've counted to three," said the leader, "One ... two ... three!"

High up above the houses, Joseph was soon drifting and dreaming with the balloon. The only sounds he could hear were the wind gently whispering and the sleepy voice of Ho-Ho in the background, saying things that he already knew but didn't know that he knew. Things like how to learn from things that happen, and we do try to learn everything we can from what happens to us ... But after we have learned all that we can, then we just save the memories in any way that we want to ... Changing the way we think about them until they don't bother us any more ... The nicest thing we can do for everyone who cares about us is to be happy ourselves ... How our own happiness makes the whole world a better place ... Happiness spreads to other people ...

How much time passed by, Joe had no idea, but he did feel better as the balloon, now over a clear blue sea, began its descent.

As Henry looked over the side, he could see that this was an island where they had never been before. Presently the balloon bumped to a halt. The place seemed deserted, with just a few rocks and some seaweed scattered about.

"Let's explore," said Ho-Ho.

They began to walk along the rocky beach, occasionally peeping into one of the many caves that the sea had dug out of the cliff face. There were all kinds of interesting seaweeds clinging to the rocks and strange gulls screeched as they flew above them. Perhaps several hours passed as the friends explored, but when they returned to the balloon, it had gone! Someone had taken away their only means of escape from the island. The friends were horrified and had no idea what could be done.

"There is someone around," said Ho-Ho, holding his trunk up and detecting something odd with his wonderful sense of smell. Sure enough, coming out of one of the caves, was an old man in a sailor's uniform, walking very slowly towards them. The friends walked towards the old man; they certainly needed all the help they could get.

"So you'll be wanting my help to get your balloon back?" the old man said, lighting a battered old pipe of tobacco. "Well, Old Seth helps them as helps Old Seth," he added.

It seemed that the old sailor himself was a prisoner on the island too. He was fishing in the waters around Petra, as the island was called, when a huge devil gull had dived onto his ship and stolen his compass. Without the compass, the old man would not dare to face the open sea.

"Old Seth knows where the devil gull's got all her treasures stored, but these old legs of mine can't climb up the likes of that," he gestured at the cliffs in the distance.

"We'll get your compass back for you," said Henry eagerly. He was a good climber and wasn't afraid of the cliffs.

"Aye," smiled the old sailor, tapping his pipe out against the rocks, "Aye, it might be that you can, but beware that devil gull. You ain't seen nothing like that evil creature. And you," he said pointing at Ho-Ho, "You'll be no good at the climb. Looks like you'll be keeping Old Seth company a while." Ho-Ho nodded; in spite of everything, there was something quite nice and friendly about the old sailor.

** **

Henry and Joe set off, armed only with a powerful torch that Old Seth had given them for the cave. The climb was hard, with few handholds and slippery areas where it would have been so easy to fall. Joe was also a superb climber and even helped Henry over the most difficult bits. The gulls continued to fly at the two friends as they neared their goal; it would have been so easy to give up and turn back.

Finally they arrived at the entrance to the devil gull's cave. The friends squirmed inside and switched on their torch. An amazing sight met their eyes and in spite of their exhaustion they gasped with astonishment. There were all kinds of valuables littered around the cave – rings, trinkets and earrings, mixed in with bottle tops, shells and pieces of glass ... but no sign of the compass! They began their search.

Suddenly a piercing cry hit the air and turning to the entrance, Henry and Joe saw the most fearsome huge bird they could ever imagine; no wonder it was called the devil gull! The two friends moved quickly together and heaved a huge boulder over the entrance to the cave. Outside, the devil gull screamed for revenge. At first the two friends were helpless and shaking with fear, but then, remembering their mission, resumed their search for the compass.

"Look at this," said Joe picking up a huge diamond, "Surely this isn't a real diamond or it would be worth a fortune!" As they shone the torch on the sparkling gem, they both became quite dazzled by it and had to look away, temporarily blinded by the bright light. Joe put it into his pocket along with an old pocket watch.

"Here it is!" said Henry, finally pulling out the compass from under a pile of beads, "This is what Old Seth wants!"

The friends surveyed the situation. They had found the compass, and Old Seth would certainly let them have their balloon to get back home, but the cries of the devil gull were becoming louder and ever angrier. Even if they made it out of the cave they would surely be knocked from the cliff by the fury of this bird.

"I've got it," said Joe after a long pause, "The diamond! The diamond! Remember how it dazzled us in this torchlight? We'll use it on the devil gull! It may well work! If we can blind the devil gull just for a few seconds we can make our escape!"

"After three," Henry whispered as they prepared to roll away the boulder, "One ... two ... three!"

They rolled the boulder away to reveal the screaming gull, who plunged furiously into the cave and into the dazzling light. For maybe 10 seconds the bird was blinded – just 10 seconds – but it was long enough to allow the friends to make their escape and to heave the boulder back over the entrance, leaving the devil gull trapped to admire her hoard forever or until such time as someone rolled the boulder away from the entrance.

Slowly but surely, with hearts light but with limbs heavy, the weary brave boys descended the cliffs down to the beach. Their fatigue made the journey even more perilous than the climb up the cliffs, but they continually helped and encouraged each other until they arrived safely on the beach.

Old Seth was overjoyed to get his compass back and so proud of the boys to have done such an amazing deed.

"So now we are all free to leave?" asked Henry. Old Seth nodded almost sorrowfully. "Old Seth got to know this island pretty well these last years, and I can tell you there be some mighty caves along the shores."

Ho-Ho and Seth had been talking all the while the boys had been gone, and both had learnt a lot. Seth had told Ho-Ho about the powers of a particular cave and Ho-Ho knew precisely what he should do to help Joseph deal with the memory of his terrifying event.

Joe stood outside the cave, thinking for a while. He had learned so much in one day. He remembered Ho-Ho talking in the balloon. He knew how important your own happiness was and how you must learn from bad experiences. He also knew that once you had learned from your bad experiences, they needn't bother you any more. Yes he could go into the cave and leave the pain behind; he stepped boldly in.

The journey back in the balloon was like a dream. Joe remembered the climbs, the devil gull and then going into Old Seth's amazing cave. In that strange cave he had re-played the old memories that had caused him so much pain. He had seen them first through a dense fog on the cave wall, like a blurred movie. Then slower, then faster, brighter and then darker, until it was all like a crumpled old photograph which was no longer needed. He had dealt with them and they were finally tucked away somewhere safe and secure in a deep recess of his mind. Finally he saw that hurt boy, the frightened Joseph, on the cave wall and reached out to him, hugged him with tears in his eyes until he knew, he knew with absolute certainty that that bad memory was just like an old half-forgotten bad dream that needn't ever bother him again. It was all over; he walked out of the cave leaving all the pain behind.

He remembered saying goodbye to Old Seth and how someday they would come back to the island of Petra. Certainly there were a lot of wonderful memories there.

Ho-Ho's voice droned on, helping and soothing, but the job had been done already and Joe knew that he could never be quite the same again.

A Problem with Water

Author's Note: this story was designed to help a particular child with bed-wetting. Should you wish to try this story to help your own child with this problem, it would help, I'm sure, to alter the details about "Nick" – the central character in the story – to fit the character of your own child. You may, of course, just read it as a normal bedtime story as it is!

There were several reasons why Henry did not enjoy the visits of his cousin Nick. Perhaps the very worst thing was that he had to give up his own bedroom and sleep in the spare room, which he didn't like at all. The reason Henry's mother gave was that his room was closest to the bathroom, which didn't seem like much of a reason to Henry. Also Nick was a very sporty boy, very good at almost all sports, especially swimming and tennis, and he was always full of energy and wanting to do things. It took a lot of energy from Henry to keep him happy.

Still, Nick was staying with Henry for a few days and there was nothing to be done. Besides, it would be nice to introduce Nick to Ho-Ho and for the three of them to have an adventure together; one of their adventures would certainly keep Nick occupied and happy, but could Henry really trust him?

Finally Henry could stand it no longer. "Can you keep a secret?" he asked Nick looking very serious, "And I don't mean just any old secret, but a very, very special secret?"

Nick looked interested, but slightly superior. "I'm in the Scouts, and we are taught lots of secret things, like how to tie secret knots and light fires without matches, so I can certainly keep any secrets you might have, Henry!"

"Very well," said Henry, suitably impressed, "I have a very special friend called Ho-Ho the elephant, who lives in a tree. When he falls down from the tree in the morning he becomes very big and sometimes wears roller-skates and we go off together having adventures and solving lots of problems."

Nick stared at Henry in amazement and disbelief. "If that were true, that would be a wonderful secret which I would certainly keep!"

"Come on, I'll show you," said Henry picking up the jug of orange juice, while Nick followed with the three glasses.

They were soon sitting underneath the damson tree, sipping their orange juice and waiting in silence. "There's no elephant!" said Nick.

"There is too," said Henry, "And he lives in this tree. I bet he is just a bit scared because he doesn't know you and he doesn't know it is OK to come down. "Ho-Ho! Ho-Ho!" Henry called out.

They waited in silence. Nothing happened. Nick smirked to himself, but, feeling a little nervous, took a small piece of flannel from his pocket and began to sniff it.

Henry was not at all worried; he had learned from his friendship with Ho-Ho that things just happen when they are ready and that there is no need to become angry or try to rush things. Once, he had told Ho-Ho how he wished he was grown up so that he could ride a big bike.

"When I was little, I thought I would never grow to be big," Ho-Ho had replied, looking very glum. Henry began to laugh at the very thought of this huge elephant worried about being small. Ho-Ho joined in, as he too could see the funny side of that particular worry! After that, Henry knew that certain things just took their time and there was no need to rush or worry about things that would happen naturally.

Suddenly there was a 'plop' and a small pink creature almost covered by the grass began to grow into a huge smiling elephant that made a child feel happy just by looking at him. Nick's eyes opened wide in astonishment.

"Ho-Ho, this is my cousin Nick," Henry said, pointing to Nick, "And this," he said waving his hand at Ho-Ho, "Is my very special friend Ho-Ho the elephant." Ho-Ho bowed and looked so funny that the two cousins began to laugh. Henry noticed what a nice laugh Nick had and wondered why he didn't laugh more often.

"What do we do now?" said Nick, looking happy but impatient.

"We just wait," said Henry, "Things will happen when they are ready."

Nick waited for a little while and then started sniffing again at the piece of flannel. Henry and Ho-Ho looked at him with great curiosity; Nick seemed too grown-up and clever to need a thing like that! After a while, Nick smiled in embarrassment and put the piece of flannel back in his pocket.

Then there was another 'plop' and a small balloon on a box-lid landed on the grass.

"What is that?" exclaimed Nick.

"Hmmm," mused Henry, "This is my Uncle Dennis' magic balloon."

Nick, of course, wanted to know everything about the balloon, but Henry just put his finger to his lips, hoping that Nick would just wait and see. They sat in silence. Henry was trying to remember how things had worked out last time.

"We all sit around the lid," he finally said, "And close our eyes and don't say anything – nothing at all whatsoever." He looked at Nick, who finally nodded in agreement.

They closed their eyes. At first nothing happened, then they noticed a strange sound, like air gushing into a tyre. Then there was a strange feeling of dizziness and floating.

"I will count to three, then we can all open our eyes together," said Henry feeling very grown-up, "One ... two ... three!"

Nick could not believe his eyes and even Henry and Ho-Ho were amazed, though they had seen this several times before. They were floating high up in the air. The small balloon had become enormous and the three of them were sitting on the lid of the box. They could still see their house, the garden and the damson tree, but they were rapidly becoming very small and disappearing into the distance.

"What's happening? Where are we going?" cried Nick, with fear in his voice, reaching into his pocket.

"We don't really know," said Henry beginning to relax and enjoy the beautiful floating feelings, "But it will all work out. You just wait and see."

Henry found it very difficult to speak, as he felt so wonderful in the balloon. His mind was full of nice pictures and feelings of being able to trust the magic balloon and where it would take them. He didn't have to worry about Nick now, as Ho-Ho would take care of that. And sure enough, Henry could hear Ho-Ho's voice, sleepily explaining about the balloon. He was telling Nick how the balloon had a mind of its own, but it was really your own mind taking you where you really needed to go, even though you didn't know yourself where you needed to go. He told him about how, when you were in the balloon, you could become really sensitive to how the balloon felt about things and so you could make sure you did the right things for it. Then he told him how the balloon could also help you learn about who you really are, and show you the things that you already know, but didn't know that you knew.

Henry looked across at Nick and noticed how much more peaceful he appeared; his face had become calmer and he looked happier in himself.

The balloon was beginning its descent and underneath there was pure blue water, the bluest blue they had ever seen.

"I don't think I will need this for much longer," said Nick sleepily, taking the flannel out of his pocket. The three friends smiled together.

Soon the balloon was nestling into the soft sand of the most beautiful beach that Nick had ever seen; it was the beach at Harmony Island. Although Henry and Ho-Ho had been there before, they were stunned by the beauty of everything they saw.

Before they could even step out of the balloon, they were surrounded by a group of small children who were clapping and waving; it was almost as if the friends had been expected!

Henry introduced Nick to the children. As usual, it was Naomi, the little girl, who did most of the talking. Apparently the mice had never come back after Henry and Ho-Ho had introduced mustard seed to the island, and indeed the people were very happy and grateful for what had happened.

"I wonder why the balloon brought us here this time?" thought Henry. "There is always a good reason for things happening the way they do!"

There on the sandy beach a group of small children and a large elephant sat in silence for a while, just enjoying each other's company.

"I wonder why we have been brought here by the balloon," said Henry. "We just love to come and visit you here on your beautiful island, but there is usually another reason for the balloon to bring us here. Do you have any problems?"

There were a few moments of silence, and then Naomi spoke out. "We do have a problem, but even you and your magic elephant cannot solve this one," she said with a sad smile.

She explained that she had been named after a beautiful flower called the Naomi flower, which only lived in one special place on the island. This was on a small plateau, very high up and almost impossible to reach. Only the fittest and thinnest of the children could climb up to the plateau, squeezing between the rocks and crevices. But high up on this plateau there had been no rain for many months and the beautiful Naomi flower was dying. Elsewhere on the island there was plenty of water, but to take water up to the Naomi flower was impossible!

"So, unless you can make it rain on the Naomi flower, you cannot help with this problem, Henry!" Naomi concluded. All the children looked very sad as Naomi recounted the story, and Henry, Ho-Ho and Nick realised just how important the Naomi flower was to the children.

They thought in silence for a while, then Henry suddenly cried out. "I've got it!" he said, leaping up excitedly. He then re-told the story of how Ho-Ho had saved Mr Scroggins' farm from the fire by carrying water in his trunk. "That's the answer," he concluded, "Ho-Ho can carry the water up the mountain in his trunk!"

The children looked from Henry to the enormous elephant, and back again at Henry, then back again to Ho-Ho and then they all began to laugh. The very idea of an enormous elephant climbing up that difficult mountain was beyond belief! Even Henry was forced to admit that, for once, Ho-Ho was not the answer!

"There must be another way," he said, thinking out loud. Nick's forehead was wrinkled in thought. He felt so much more powerful after the balloon journey, so much stronger and more confident, that he felt confident about finding an answer.

"What are you thinking, Nick?" asked Henry.

"I was thinking that if children had trunks like Ho-Ho, we could easily get the water up the mountain!" The children all laughed at the very idea of children having trunks instead of noses.

"But we do have mouths!" added Nick. The children all looked at Nick with great interest. "If we take buckets of water as near as possible to the plateau, then fill up our mouths and climb the last bit, we can empty the water in our mouths onto the Naomi plants. How much water will they need, Naomi?"

Naomi looked amazed. "I think just two or three full buckets of water would do it. That's a lot of children's mouths, but there are eight of us who can make the climb, and with Henry and Nick, that would make ten of us. It might take us half a day, and it would be exhausting, but it might well work!"

Her eyes shone with excitement and the children rapidly began their preparations.

With great difficulty three buckets of water were taken up the mountain as high as they could manage. Then, one at a time, each of the ten children who could make the climb filled their mouths with water. Nick felt thrilled that his idea had been accepted by the children; this was even better than his adventures in the Scouts.

The climb was incredibly difficult and at first even Nick found it impossible to hold the water in his mouth while climbing hard and wriggling through the narrow places. Each time, however, he improved. It seemed that his mouth could hold more water if he held it in a certain way, and with practice he managed to keep his lips pressed tightly together so that none of the water leaked out. When he had started he had been the worst of all the children, but he was so desperate to help that he was finally the very best. It seemed that his mouth had even increased in size! He had learned how to relax his body for the climb so that the tension in his mouth didn't spill the water, and how to keep his mind comfortable even though the climb was so hard and so hot. He was desperate for his plan to work and made more journeys and carried more water than anyone else.

Finally the job was done. The flowers had their roots watered and were already starting to look better. The children sat round the flowers, hot and exhausted but very happy and contented. Nick looked from the happy children to the beautiful Naomi flowers he had helped to save, and he knew that he would treasure that moment for the rest of his life.

** **

As the balloon floated away from the island, Nick felt truly wonderful. "I really don't need my flannel any more," he said, "Do you and Ho-Ho want it?"

"What do you think, Ho-Ho?" asked Henry.

Ho-Ho thought for a moment. "If Nick doesn't need the flannel, then it can still be good for him to keep it, to remind him of all the things he has done."

"Yes, that's right," thought Nick, as he began to dream with the movements of the balloon. He enjoyed the feelings of friendship, a sense of belonging and feeling wonderful about himself as a person.

Ho-Ho was talking in his simple elephant-talk, telling stories about a miller and his windmill and how the wind turned the sails of the windmill, grinding the wheat. He explained how the miller and the windmill were much like the balloon and the three friends, as even in his sleep the miller knew what the windmill was doing. But Nick felt that much of him was still on the island, still there on the sand where Naomi gave him the Naomi flower to take away with him and, blushing, she had kissed him on the cheek. He held the Naomi flower and knew that this hadn't been a dream, but that what he had learnt this day would be always with him and he would never feel lonely and frightened ever again. Henry knew that something very important had happened to Nick, that his problem was somehow no longer there and from now on they would be very good friends indeed.

In fact they had many more adventures together in the future, but for some reason Nick never needed to take Henry's bedroom any more ...